SURVIVE

OR DIE

JOHN McGAULEY

Contents

1

CHARACTER LIST AND DEDICATION

Characters

Marcus Wayne - A former Sheriff from King James County, Georgia. Husband to Maggie Wayne, and the two had a son together. His name is Connor Wayne.

Maggie Wayne-Wife and mother to Marcus Wayne, and before the apocalypse, she was a stay-at-home mom who took their son to school and picked him up.

Connor Wayne- Son of Marcus and Maggie Wayne, was only eight years old when the apocalypse happened, and the world went to hell.

Randall Walsh- Marcus's best friend since childhood, and the two are sheriffs at the same department at King James County Sheriff Department.

Carter Dixon- Former Atlanta SWAT member during the apocalypse, he served and protected the city of Atlanta. When the dead entered the city, he fought them dead until the town was overrun—also a hunter and a skilled tracker.

Philip Scott (The Warden): Former Saint Louis Prison Warden and former mayor. (mentioned)

Martha Dixon: Sister to Carter and an excellent hunter and tracker like her brothers.

Atticus Dixon: Brother to Martha and Carter, a skilled hunter and tracker.

Richard Wayne (Mentioned): Brother of Marcus Wayne

Madison Wayne (Mentioned): Sister to both Marcus and Richard Wayne.

Ian Wayne (Mentioned): Grandfather of Marcus, Richard, and Madison Wayne served in World War II and the Korean War.

Joshua: Friend to Marcus Wayne and Randall, served in the same department together and graduated with them at the academy the same year.

Kyle: Former Deputy and a friend to Marcus Wayne, Randall Walsh, and Joshua.

Scott Walsh: (mentioned, brother to Randall Walsh deceased.)

Lucas: a survivor who escaped the Saint Louis Prison, a former scout for the community.

Dedication

I would like to dedicate this book two people in my life that have been special to me, the first is my grandmother Nancy Anna Corcoran and my friends as well as my teachers.

2

PROLOGUE

Pro-

logue

The police cruiser was parked in the parking lot as the two deputies were busy eating the meal they had ordered from the restaurant. These officers have been friends since they were children; they joked and shared stories of the past and recent events in the news.

"So, Marcus, how are you and Maggie doing?" said the officer in the front passenger seat of the police cruiser; Marcus paused before answering as he finished chewing the spaghetti and meatballs he ordered. He politely wiped his lips with the napkin and drank some water before speaking to his partner, who was eagerly waiting for him to answer his question.

"She's good, a great wife, and we talk a lot about the future of our son Connor. We argued last night; she must have had a dreadful day at work or something because she just had this attitude that I have not seen in such a long time." Said Marcus as he still felt the hurt from the argument last night about the house they were living in and if they wanted to renovate the home. The house they lived in King James County, Georgia, was built after the second world war and had various problems. Marcus was pushing for it to be renovated, while Maggie was pushing for them to move.

"Yeah, I argued with my girlfriend last night, man." Said the officer as he was trying to move away from a subject that still caused Marcus to have just a little shift in mood.

"Yeah, what was it about Randall?" said Marcus as he turned his head to his friend and partner; Randall nodded his head and had a little flare of emotion since he was still angry about it.

"She was asking me if she and I were going to marry. I do not know if I want that with this woman, man; listen, she's great and everything, but she is just too fucking stupid sometimes. She is always in my business and asking about shit that does not matter in my world; she told me last night that she wanted you and Maggie to have a family. Then when I was done with the conversation, she forgot to turn off the damn lights in the family room and the kitchen; I had to turn them off the lights because she is damn stupid even to know where the light switch is, which we had another argument and had her damn father's preacher voice." Said Randall as he chuckled and turned his head to see Marcus laughing and trying not to choke on the food he was trying to eat.

"So, what was your reply to her preacher's voice?"

"I wanted to tell her, listen, this is my house, and if you leave the lights on, then I have to pay the power bill bitch."

"You didn't say that did you?" said Marcus as there was a pause, Randall was thinking of last night, and he replied.

"No, I went with the southern gentleman's way of speaking that, and she went to sleep; I came to find out she was drinking my beer and was drunk like it was a bachelor party." Randall, the two of them laughed; however, the laughter stopped when dispatch went through on the radio.

"We have armed assailants at the King James County bank, requesting any available officers to respond." Said the female officer working at dispatch. As soon as hearing the news, Randall and Marcus gathered their food and placed it back into the paper bag to be thrown away as their drinks. Marcus turned the keys in the ignition and started to drive off as Randall threw the food and beverages inside the bag into the trash can to their right near the entrance; as Marcus went to the police cruiser, Randall placed his bulletproof vest on him. Marcus drove the police cruiser as the sirens wailed and were moving at high speed towards the bank, which was in an active armed robbery; he looked into the rearview mirror as he saw three more police cars that were Sheriff Deputies. They followed Marcus as he drove. Marcus stopped once they reached the bank and exited the police cruiser as he joined the massive blue blockade of the town; Marcus noticed that the Atlanta Swat was on scene and US Marshals, as well as other counties, were there surrounding the bank. Randall Welsch and Marcus Wayne were behind their police cruiser. The armed bank robbers opened fire with a massive barrage of automatic and assault rifle weaponry toward the police, who took cover immediately. Marcus Wayne checked his Colt Python Magnum to see if his gun was loaded in the revolver cylinder and if the bullets' back end was in the cylinder, ready to be used. The law enforcement officers counted silently in their heads as the armed bank robbers fired their guns, which were higher caliber rounds from military-grade weapons. Marcus, Randall, and the other law enforcement officers knew that these people were either former military or former law enforcement officers. Marcus looked at the SWAT teams equipped with MP5 submachine guns, M16s, and shotguns; they looked slow with their body armor and bulletproof vests. The barrage coming from the bank lasted what seemed like hours until there was silence as the armed robbers began to reload; at that moment, SWAT made its move and began to throw smoke grenades to conceal their movements and confuse the criminals.

"Come on, you fucking pigs, you want to die. We still have plenty of ammo left for all you blue bastards!" shouted a criminal from the bank's window as he was busy reloading his Ak-47.

As the smoke began to fill the police line, they moved under cover of the white smoke closer to the bank built during the Civil War. Marcus Wayne, Randall Welsch, and Joshua followed behind the SWAT teams as they moved toward the bank's front entrance. The officers could smell the inside of the bank, which had a strong odor of both deaths as well as spent ammunition, followed by the smell of blood that was thick in the air; these criminals were bloodthirsty thugs who would waste no time in killing anyone that got in there a way or were witnesses. Slowly the smoke began to clear as the officers stopped taking cover behind the brink wall of the bank that was full of bullet holes when the first officers arrived to stop the armed criminals; the detectives would later discover some to be from the criminals as they shot at the security guards who stood at the front doors, the bodies of the security guards were lying next to the door. Some were on the steps with blood still coming from the open wounds. Joshua slowly moved away from the cover, thinking he could catch the criminals by surprise, and before he could fire, a quick succession of shots was fired; it sounded like three shots. The three bullets hit Joshua, each penetrating a different body part. Marcus and the other officers watched in horror as Joshua fell dead with three bullet holes, one of them hit his bulletproof vest, and the other two killed him. One bullet penetrated his head and the other through his throat; Marcus and the others remained covered as swat began to toss smoke grenades to obscure their movements. They heard the helicopters' approach, news helicopters, and some Police moving towards the bank. The criminals were highly trained, possibly from the former military, and were professionals in their profession as thugs. Marcus and the other officers moved into the bank, as the bank became a battlefield between law enforcement and the bank robbers. Marcus fired his Colt Python Magnum, hitting a masked bank robber with a tattoo on his left hand, a prison gang tattoo. The bank robber Marcus had shot was hit in the chest, hitting him in his right lung; Marcus walked over and kicked the gun away from the robber, who didn't care to ask for his name, nor did he understand why he was doing this. Marcus leveled his revolver to his eye as he aimed the gun to kill the criminal for revenge for killing his fellow officer; the bank lobby was a mess as the sounds of gunfire created so much noise that you felt like your head was going to explode. Marcus, before he could fire his gun turned his head sharply to see another robber standing behind his cover and fired two bullets that hit Marcus with such force it caused him to step back; one of the bullets hit Marcus in his vest, and the other hit him in the right shoulder as he turned from the force of impact. Marcus groaned and moaned in pain as he used his left hand to fill where the second bullet hit him, only to feel blood coming from the wound; Marcus used the strength in his right arm to fire his revolver, hitting the robber, who shot in the throat and killing him.

"Officer down!" shouted Randall but fired his shotgun as he headed over to the wounded officer only to find that it was Marcus, his best friend; Randall grabbed his friend's collar as he, dragged Marcus behind a desk, and checked on his friend to see that he was shot. Randall conducted first aid on his best friend and unbuttoned Marcus's shirt to see that one of the bullets hit Marcus's vest, and he was struggling to catch his breath.

"Hey man, keep trying to get your breath, man. You're going to be fine." Said Randall as he saw that Marcus hit his shoulder as blood slowly flowed from the open wound; around the bank, it was chaos. Randall placed his right and left hands on one another to keep pressure on the gunshot wound to Marcus's right shoulder as he saw another officer come with a first aid kit placing gauze around Marcus's right shoulder. Randall stayed with Marcus as they moved the wounded officer away from the shootout. Randall provided cover as an officer, and a swat officer dragged Marcus outside the lobby into the massive police presence. Randall fired his shotgun, hitting a robber with an AK-47 and watching the shotgun shells penetrate the man as blood and bone exploded from the gaping hole in the man's chest. Randall heard gunfire slowly dying as the remaining bank robbers were pushed back from the lobby into the bank faults as the officers continued to pursue the criminal thugs.

"It sounds like things will be wrapping up soon." said a paramedic to Randall, who was watching Marcus being loaded into the ambulance that they stopped as the officers who stayed behind their cars joined the shootout in the bank against the criminals. Randall knelt beside his friend Marcus as the paramedics continued to check Marcus's oxygen levels and if there was an exit wound. Randall ignored the paramedic who spoke to him as he saw Marcus remove the oxygen mask from his face.

"Randall, please don't tell my wife about this; I don't want her to worry. This stays between us; promise me, Randall." Said Marcus as he saw a brief hesitation in Randall's reply.

"Okay, Marcus, I promise." Said Randall as Marcus and the gurney he was on were lifted into the ambulance. Randall watched as Marcus was loaded into the ambulance, and police officers helped move some of their cars to allow the wounded officer a clear exit to the hospital; Randall ran with his shotgun in his right hand to the police cruiser that he and his partner drove to the armed robbery call to follow his friend to the hospital.

After what seemed like four hours when it was three hours, the armed robbers were either subdued permanently or surrendered to be placed in handcuffs for the courts to determine their fate. Randall and the King James County Sheriff's department waited at the hospital for Marcus Wayne to come out of surgery or for a doctor to deliver the bad news. Randall, like Marcus, didn't believe in God, and that day he decided to pray to whoever would listen as the morning became afternoon and the afternoon began to creep into the evening. Randall sat down on a chair and looked at his hands to see that he still had the dried blood of his best friend; Randall fought back the emotions that were swelling in his soul that wanted him to cry and feel something as if it was his fault that his best friend was injured in the line of duty. It felt like hours, no centuries waiting in the waiting room as his friend lay in surgery, fighting for his life. Randall heard the sound of a kid's footsteps and a woman's heels walking through the hallway to the waiting room to the left of the metal door that read on a sign, restricted authorized personnel only. Randall and the other officers turned their heads to see Maggie Wayne with her son Connor Wayne enter the waiting room. She walked over to Randall, still trying to process what had occurred; Maggie had mixed emotions of sadness and grief, and anger on her face.

"Maggie, you shouldn't be here with Connor. You two need the rest, please he is still in surgery, and we don't know anything that has occurred beyond those doors. Marcus told me not to tell because he didn't want to worry you; I promised that it would stay between us. Who told you?"

"A nurse called me when I was in the car with Connor from school, and it took us forever to get here because of the heavy police presence outside the hospital. I heard at work about the armed robbery at the bank in the center of town; it's okay; I know that you officers have your badge of honor about not speaking certain things. Is Marcus, okay?"

"I don't know, Mrs. Wayne; I know when he was being placed into the ambulance, he lost consciousness enroute to the hospital, and by the time I arrived, the nurse told me that it was bad and he may not make it off the table. I'm so sorry, Mrs. Wayne and Maggie. I'm sorry I can't process this. It happened all too fast; we went into the bank lobby and were fine. Then, one second later, Marcus was down. It should be me inside that room, not him, it's my job to protect him like he was my other brother, and I didn't protect him." Said Randall Welsch as his emotions were getting the better of him and his mind was trying to process everything that had transpired; Maggie hugged Randall trying to shut him up as she struggled to fight back the tears coming from her eyes. A female officer and a male officer distracted Connor from what transpired to go to the playroom, where their toys and board games kept children from adult conversations. The metal doors that led to the surgery center opened to reveal a surgeon wearing a bloodstained lab coat from Marcus's successful surgery. The surgeon entered the room and saw the gathered officers and a woman whom he was told to be Maggie Wayne, Marcus's wife "Officer Welsch, Mrs. Wayne. Your friend and husband did great, and we managed to stop the bleeding, repair the damage, and extract the bullet fragments. But if Marcus suffers any pain from the surgery, he will be placed into a medicated coma until he has recovered. Officer Wayne will be transported to his room and come back tomorrow when you can see him, and you don't want to see him with all these tubes that are correctly present. Some codes happened when we were there, he had to get fresh blood to circulate into his system and plasma, and he did great, but there were some close calls." Said the Surgeon, who walked away after Officer Welsch and Maggie Wayne, as well as the other officers, replied with their gratitude. Randall took Maggie Wayne and Connor Wayne home to get some rest.

Randall arrived at the Wayne household and parked his police cruiser on the curb as he would watch over Marcus's family for the night. Randall took off his belt and his boots as he grabbed a blanket to make his bed on the couch; he sat on the couch and turned on the tv to see that the midnight news was speaking about Marcus Wayne, the sheriff's deputy who was wounded in the line of duty. Randall switched channels to the national news talking about something that occurred three hours ago, an incident in Los Angeles, California; Randall listened to the news anchor speaking about the incident in Los Angeles, California, of a gang war within the poorer part of LA.

"Police arrived at the scene of what they expected to be dead bodies in the aftermath of a gang war; however, they were greatly disturbed to see that the bodies they were expecting to find were not there. Detectives were confused, and after they arrived, the police heard gunshots followed by screaming when they arrived on the scene, they saw a man eating someone. Officers tried to detain the cannibal and were forced to use deadly force. Please, please; I am getting some breaking news from our English affiliate." The female news anchor paused as she touched her left ear, and the screen switched to a news journalist in England; behind the news, the journalist was a police presence with crime scene tape.

"Are we live? Okay, we are living." The news journalist said in a British accent; Randall noticed he was nervous about what had occurred.

"Good evening, just behind me earlier today in the city of Dover. Police responded to an incident where a man and a woman were eating the shop owner, at which point police used nonlethal tactics to subdue the man and woman. I heard from an officer earlier that one of the responding officers was bitten on the arm and is currently in hospital. We were told that shortly before we arrived on the scene, the armed officers you see maintain the crowd opened fire on the man and woman who were eating the shop owner and biting an officer. I interviewed a witness that the police fired seventeen rounds of ammunition into the two suspects, and they got back up; with the seventeenth shot, the head killed them. Police are not ruling out this was a bad batch of some drug. We will update you when more news arrives; Something seems off about what has transpired in England and California before I sign off. "Said the English news journalist; Randall turned off the tv and took off his shirt and pants. Once Randall stripped his clothes, he covered himself with the blanket and fell asleep.

3

Chapter 1

King James County Hospital, 2010

Three months and two weeks later

Randall Welsch, dressed in his uniform, walked into the hospital to visit his friend; things were changing as this disease spread worldwide. Randall noticed that even in King James County, there were preparations as business owners and businesses placed boards onto the windows. Randall passed by nurses and doctors who were either in deep conversation or were in a hurry to the patients in the hospital; Randall had taken turns with Marcus's wife, Maggie, to visit Marcus, who was placed into a medicated coma. Randall Welsch and everyone in the world had seen that things were getting bad, riots had broken out over police shootings, and lootings had broken out as the criminals were taking advantage of the chaos. Randall turned right through the hallway and passed a nurse's station who were busy at work, and some even looked nervous. As Randall walked through the hallways, he heard medical codes being barked through the intercom as nurses and doctors sprinted through the hall to emergencies. Randall held in his hand a couple of flowers for his friend to be placed in his room and a get-well-soon card. He hated this and missed his friend; he was shot last year in 2009, and he should have recovered or, better yet, healed. Randall rounded the last corner, approached Marcus's room, and entered out of politeness, even though his friend wouldn't respond. Randall Welsch opened the door and closed it behind him as he placed the flowers into a cup and put his get well soon card next to the cup; he grabbed a chair near the dresser and sat looking at his friend.

"Listen, man, and things have gotten worse since 2009. You've probably heard it on the news whenever the nurses are in here to check your meds and give you food. I should be in that bed instead of you; there have been riots and lootings. I've been looking out for your son, a scared man. He needs his dad. Your wife Maggie is scared, and I've been watching over her as well, don't worry if things go bad. I'll take care of them, man; keep them safe." As Randall sat on the chair talking to his friend, who knew he heard his every word, the room was quiet except for the beeping of the heart monitor and the sounds of the machines breathing for him. Randall stood up from the chair and walked to the window as he saw a helicopter fly overhead that appeared to be a military helicopter; Randall knew things were slowly getting worse. He turned to his friend Marcus, knowing he was doing a good thing by keeping his family safe.

"Marcus, man, please, if you can hear me. It would be best if you woke up soon; this world needs your leadership and bravery. I'll hold the line until you return; we will need Marcus Wayne, whatever comes next. Get well, man; love you, brother." Said Randall as he walked out of the door and closed it behind him, leaving the hospital.

After leaving the hospital, Randall Welsch drove his car to King James County Sheriff's station; he listened to his car's radio as a news station spoke about a riot breaking out in Saint Louis as this disease spread worldwide. The radio broadcast was interrupted by an emergency alert that sounded almost like a tornado siren; Randall listened intently as the broadcaster was replaced with the President's voice as he spoke to the nation on the ongoing situation.

"My fellow Americans, I know things are scary right now as the threat of disease has spread throughout our great cities and our great country. But members of my party and across the aisle have come together as Americans; effective today, the United States military will establish safe zones within many cities and provide security and safety to your neighborhoods. My friends, my fellow Americans, my fellow Republicans, and my friends across the aisle. Now is not the time for us to fight one another but to fight as one voice and nation. I have spoken to our country's greatest minds; our scientists have been working with other nations to study this disease and its symptoms. The CDC is working tirelessly on its research on the disease and hoping to find a vaccine. We as one nation can do incredible things when we stand together; this is the opportunity for as long as this disease threatens our world and our nation. We will fight as one voice, nation, flag, and most of all, as Americans. I will address the nation with further information whenever I receive it, and we are in this fight together." The President of the United States radio addressed the nation for the first time since the outbreak.

Randall was stunned as he was driving at hearing the president speak that the United States military would begin deployment into various cities throughout the United States. Randall was right that things were getting worse, slowly getting worse, blood would flow even more, and chaos would reign in the streets. Randall arrived at the sheriff's station and turned off the car before stepping out to see that other officers had heard the news and the civilians who worked at the department had. Everyone stopped when they heard helicopters flying in the air. Everyone either worked on their police cruiser or returned to the station to go home, looking to the sky above to see military helicopters flying. The thoughts in everyone's mind came into being that things were going from bad to worse. The end would begin to follow, and like the Roman Empire years before the United States, the collapse started slow, and things began to pick up.

Atlanta

Georgia

The Georgian national guard rolled into the city of Atlanta, Georgia, without further warning from the Governor's office; they began establishing checkpoints and erecting barbed wire. Staff Sergeant Dunn dressed in his combat uniform and walked the perimeter of the forward operating base, which was found. Staff Sergeant Dunn had served two tours in Iraq and Afghanistan and had seen things that ordinary people would hopefully never see. However, Dunn was beginning to convince himself that things were getting worse and going to get worse. When he returned home from his deployment, his commanding officer told him he was being deployed along with the rest of the military. He was surprised to have said that he would be deployed in the United States in an effort by the military to show the citizens that they had a hold on the issues at hand. Dunn had seen the news from the early reports of an outbreak; he was shocked that something like this was happening. It felt like a bad horror movie or was a practical joke taken too far. Dunn remembered listening to news agencies on the internet in 2009 discussing that this outbreak would blow over, that Police all over the world were ruling this as a bad batch of drugs. However, Dunn was no scientist, but something felt significantly off about how in one news report, the Police opened fire on the man tearing the flesh out of a woman who accidentally hit him with her car but killed him. Police in Kansas City responded to the call of an accident where a woman in her car accidentally shot a young college student riding his bike and killed him. When Police arrived, they had paramedics on the scene who tried to render aid to the young college student. From what Dunn recalled hearing and reading, the young college student grabbed the paramedic doing CPR by the back of his head and pulled his neck towards his mouth as he tore flesh from his neck.

Dunn, according to the Police action statement and news report, the Officers grabbed the paramedic who was just bitten on the channel away from the college student. The student got back up and took eighteen rounds in his chest, legs, arms, shoulder, and neck, but to no effect; eventually, officers reloaded their handguns and fired another wave of bullets, but only one round with the aim of the officer went into the student's skull killing him. Already Dunn was overhearing from the scientists in the CDC that these people who died in an accident or any form of death came back as if nothing happened, the word that he heard scientists causing the return of the dead as zombies. Something was happening that they were having trouble explaining. Dunn stopped pacing around the fenced perimeter of the

CDC building that he was guarding, where he saw a four-door sedan arrive at the front checkpoint gate.

Dunn kept his rifle ready to know it was a scientist reporting to work. Index finger hovering above the safety in case he needed to switch it off. Dunn felt hot in his uniform as the sun was beating down on him; they had a briefing when they arrived in Atlanta, where their first mission was to provide safety and security. The main objective of the United States military and the globe was to try to prevent the further spread of this disease. He recalled from an earlier briefing that Russian scientists were en route to Cuba to help the Cuban scientist working on a vaccine to quell the infection. Dunn knew that things were growing desperate, and it was only to get worse. The scientist left the checkpoint after the guard cleared his ID and allowed him through the complex; Dunn wanted this disease to be crushed and things to return to normal. Dunn continued to walk the perimeter and listen to the radio chatter as some of the soldiers were patrolling the city of Atlanta; Dunn felt a little ashamed that the United States military within these safe zones would help the police departments with local law enforcement issues.

4

CHAPTER 2

As the sun rose across the globe, a year passed, and things were getting worse; in 2009, just a few incidents turned into outbreaks. Nations quickly deployed their military to quell the spreading of infection, and violence broke out worldwide. The religions of the world struggled to make sense of what was occurring; many called this God's punishment on the earth for falling so low and turning to the whims of the Devil; others called it the beginning of the End times and that the son of man was returning to the world to judge his creation. The governments of the world, specifically those that practiced dictatorship and socialism as well as communism, fought together as their scientists worked on a vaccine as well as a cure to reverse the infection; the Chinese military launched missiles into their cities as well as attacked its neighbors, blaming them for the outbreak of the disease. American and European news channels spoke about how Chinese forces were in a ground war in Vietnam and India, threatening to conquer them; their justification was the outbreak of the disease that scientists named T1S1-19 codenamed in a science forest fire. The nations that fell to the dead were Iran, New Zealand, Iraq, Syria, Saudi Arabia, United Arab Emirates, Iceland, Greenland, Hawaii, Guam, Philippines, Kuwait, Laos, Cambodia, Chile, Jamaica, Ethiopia, and Ireland. The remaining nations called those that had died from the disease the infected, but many years later, those that were surviving would call the dead walkers, biters, corpses, bloaters, rotters, monsters, and many other names. In the United States, cities burned as riots and looting continued as the military struggled to maintain order. In the town of King James County, Georgia, the doctors at the hospital were beginning evacuation under the demands of the national guard as they tried to hold off a massive horde of the infected. The doctors, including Randall Welsch, Marcus's childhood friend and patrol partner, waited in the room as doctors checked on their patient to see if he was waking up from his coma. Once they finished their physical evaluation of Marcus Wayne, he got up and, with a nurse's aide, helped him get dressed. Randall Welsch stood outside his friend's door and noticed from the third-floor patient window that he saw the thousands of zombies approaching the city in the distance.

"Whatever you're doing, doctors, I don't mean to sound pushing, but you must do it fast. It looks like the national guard have begun to create a kill zone and are opening fire on the infected." Randall pointed with his right index finger to the window as the national guard kept a defensive perimeter within the town. Their snipers also coordinated mortar strikes on the infected; the earth shook as the shells slammed into the soil. The infected that were hit by the mortar shells either lost their legs or were blown apart; the armored personnel carriers opened fire with their fifty-caliber shells into the dead. The ground was being slowly drowned in blood as the dead were cut down, and the national guard all over the United States was busy fighting off the massive hordes of the infected they called them. In the cities that remained in the United States began mass evacuations of doctors, scientists, government officials, judges, west point graduates, naval academy graduates, private military, corporate officials, historians, journalists, and high-ranking military officials along with their families were moved through the long lines to board the waiting aircraft that would take them to a top-secret base. In Saint Louis, Missouri, the Missouri national guard struggled to contain the horde of the infected who broke through the fences and began to tear people apart. In San Francisco, the same thing continued as the dead broke through the walls and the screams as people were being torn apart. The cries of the people terrified even that of the national guard who was struggling to defend themselves and those who were essential to get their ticket of evacuation to the front of the lines. All over the world, the last news broadcasts before the camera stopped rolling were the same message; this is the end and a message of hope that someday humanity would rise from the darkness. Local television and radio repeated other letters across the world's cities.

"Help is on its way; please stand by. Please keep your doors locked and wait for an officer to escort you to the nearest airport for evacuation; please don't panic and be afraid because help is on its way." The male's voice on the radio repeated in a loop in the airwaves throughout the United States; however, as things were getting worse for them to handle, the United States military began turning off the power and blanketing the cities in darkness.

Randall Welsch, dressed in his uniform, walked over to his friend Marcus who was dressed in some clothes that his wife Maggie Wayne left behind for him.

"Hey man, it is good to see you again. But I would be grateful if you could listen to me, and I will help you leave this place and go to your family. There has been an outbreak; people are eating each other, and things are worse; there is no time to explain, but we need to move." As Randall tried his best to sound diplomatic, Randall took point as a nurse placed Marcus into a wheelchair and rolled him to a staff-only elevator. The doctors in the room had scattered as they ran to help with other patients; Randall kept his right-hand hovering over his holster in case something happened. The staff-only elevator took them to the underground garage, where staff parked their cars, and Randall brought Marcus's wife and son, who were happy to see Marcus awake but also appearing to look better than he did. Randall got into the driver's seat and helped the nurse load Marcus into the passenger seat; inside Maggie's bag was Marcus's old uniform, gun, watch, and sheriff hat. Randall Welsch heard the thumps as gunfire echoed throughout the whole building, and the screams; he knew that the security staff in the hospital were having difficulty containing what was occurring. The nurse quickly ran away, leaving the wheelchair behind as she ran to the elevator to help people; Randall felt the nurse would not return. Randall drove away as Marcus asked his wife what was going on, still groggy from his long sleep and his wife explained to Marcus what happened when he was in the hospital. He drove out of the town away from the hospital, turned left then right, and was breaking the law for the speed limit. Randall knew that he couldn't leave his friend Marcus to die in that hospital; behind him, he saw through the rearview mirror as the dead continued into the town, and the military was losing many of them being taken down by the dead chucks from them.

Randall stopped at the overpass of the highway that pointed towards Atlanta and pulled the car to the side to see King James County in flames as the military conducted its contingency protocol. The military protocol was that if things got way out of hand, the military would drop napalm and bomb the city or town if it fell to the dead, regardless of those not infected. Randall began to tear up as he watched fighter jets and bombers drop payloads onto the town, he called home; he placed his arms to the back of his head, powerless to stop the bombs from falling. Randall stood there as memories flashed through his head when his parents were alive, and his brother Scott Welsch died when he was very young. Maggie got out of the back passenger seat and was speechless, watching the military bomb the town as the screams echoed of those that were innocent civilians.

"Oh my God, there bombing the city. But so many people aren't infected and trying to survive like everybody is."

"Son of a bitch, this isn't happening. This is a bad dream, and this isn't happening." As Randall was trying to process what was occurring, he stopped and turned his head to see an old truck and two motorcycles that stopped as three people got out of their vehicles. Randall, who was outside his truck, and Marcus stepped out of the car wearing a t-shirt and cargo pants to see a swat officer with two other people who seemed like outdoors people. Randall and Marcus saw two males and one female; the more prominent male still wore his Swat uniform without body armor. The other man next to him wore what a typical hunter would wear as well as the female.

"I'm sheriff deputy Randall Welsch of the King James County Sheriff's Department. Are you three okay? Is anyone bitten or scratched?" Randall said as he placed his hand onto his holstered pistol, unsure about the situation.

"I was just about to ask you the same question; I'm former Atlanta Swat of Atlanta Police Department Carter Dixon. This is my brother Atticus Dixon and my sister Martha Dixon; I guess we are attracting much attention from the survivors in your town." Said Carter as he pointed his thumb behind him to see car headlights, Carter and his siblings were a bit nervous after what was occurring in Atlanta . The city was being overrun, and the evacuations had stopped; the national guard was stranded after their pilots took off for wherever their destination took them. Carter had been in the city fighting with other swat officers as the dead entered the town; he looked to his siblings, who were hunters but also worked various jobs. Atticus was imprisoned daily because of his drug addiction issues and killing their abusive father three years ago. Martha was a hunter and skilled tracker but was once an undercover cop; she was a tough woman and worked in the same station as her brother Carter.

"Nice to meet you; that is my best friend and patrol partner, Marcus Wayne. His wife, Maggie Wayne, and their son Connor Wayne." Said Randall Welsch as he defused the situation seeing that people were on the ground; other people arrived and parked.

"We need to find a place to stay and get our things in order; we should go for Atlanta ." Marcus was unaware of what was happening in the city eleven miles away.

"We just came there; we thought up north would be better. But clearly, it isn't, and the roads are jammed up on the highways and the freeways. We have a cabin in this park that is a good distance from Atlanta and seventeen miles away from the city." Replied Carter as he saw that Marcus was trying to piece what was going on in his head, he heard about him on the local news. He was injured on duty in a shootout with bank robbers.

"Marcus Wayne, as in the sheriff who was shot in 2009 on a bank robbery call." Martha was piecing together the name and where she heard the word. Marcus nodded and got out of the passenger seat, feeling almost naked without his gun belt around his waist.

"Okay, listen up, anyone who wants to get away from this place. You can come with us to a campsite seventeen miles from here; we can regroup and think about our next steps. I knew we didn't know each other and were only strangers two years ago, but now we have to stick with each other and fight this until our scientific minds figure something out. The military will be returning for us, and we will regroup while we wait for them to return." Randall, who was taking up being a leader; he and Marcus walked to Carter, who went to his truck to pull out a map where he marked the campsite and what roads were jammed. Once everyone kept the same, they drove from the overpass and headed south, away from the town in flames. Marcus sat in the backseat with his wife and son, who were also scared of what was happening; he only woke up from his coma to find that the world he was shot in was gone; the dead walked the world.

The car ride took an hour to two hours to arrive at the location, and the morning sky turned to the afternoon sky. Those following Randall's truck ended up in the old RV campsite to find that they were the only ones there, except for an abandoned RV parked on the grounds. Marcus and Randall, and the Dixon siblings exited their vehicles as they walked around checking the cabins with weapons at the ready. Marcus and Randall checked a cabin by the ranger's office; Marcus still felt the pain from his injury as he moved, checking corners and rooms. Once the two of them cleared the cabin, they moved outside to see that everyone was getting ready to find a place to sleep for the evening. Marcus holstered his colt python and walked over to help his wife and son find their cabin; he was new to this new world. Some people tried their cell phones to reach family members but received no signal or static; the only thing playing on the radio was the same message on repeat.

Marcus checked a cabin while his wife and son waited outside; once it was clear, he allowed them inside, where they set their bedding and clothes in the dresser. Marcus helped unpack his wife's stuff and pulled a book out from the suitcases; in which he sat down on a chair to see it was their family book full of photos of their wedding day and vacations. Maggie Wayne stopped and looked at her husband as he flipped through the pages; she smiled at him and remembered why she fell in love. Maggie Wayne was a white woman; her family raised her to be a good Christian and were business owners who treated their employees well. She was a stay-at-home mom when Marcus was in the police force; she was a brunette who loved her son Connor and her husband completely.

"I couldn't leave our memories behind in our house, and when you were in the coma, there was so much looting and crime that people were scared. I prayed for your return to our son and me because I was going through hell without." Said Maggie Wayne as she teared up, and Marcus closed the book as he walked towards her with the wooden floors creaking. Marcus wrapped his arms around her and kissed her gently on the lips, they both smiled, and he gently moved some hair aside to look at her.

"You don't have to be worried anymore; it will take much getting used to what happened. We have to hold onto our humanity; that is how we beat this, and if there are other survivors out there, we have to fight the dead together. We survive this by pulling together, not apart; we survive or die. That's the rule now." Said Marcus to his wife, who nodded; he wiped some tears from her face knowing that she was still scared. Marcus and Maggie Wayne helped their son unpack his stuff and then decided to go to bed.

5

CHAPTER 3

Marcus Wayne woke up in the early morning and left the cabin after getting dressed to see that Randall was dressed in brown cargo pants and a gray t-shirt showing off his muscular body.

"Morning."

"Morning, man, we missed you during dinner. I suppose you were still tired after the ordeal yesterday."

"Yeah, I was Randall, so what are we doing today?"

"You and I are returning to King James County to gather supplies like food or water, maybe some guns from the station, and ammo. We need medicine and stuff in case people get hurt." Said Randall as he placed his 9mm handgun into his holster and checked his shotgun before cocking the gun to place a round in the chamber. Marcus was wearing his old sheriff uniform and hat; he conducted his ritual as he checked his Colt Python Magnum before placing it into his holster. It was a week since things had fallen apart, and Marcus struggled to understand what was going on even after he woke up from the coma. Randall would help Marcus understand that the dead were the threat; he needed to know that these things weren't people anymore. The two got into Randall's truck and drove out of their small camp, the sun was still rising in the sky, and it was nothing but quiet as the two headed to where they grew up.

Carter and his siblings got up as well shortly after Marcus and Randall left to see that the people who had joined the group were waking up as well; Carter put on his old biker vest that had an eagle on the back and his club's name written on the back as well. He was one tough man and a forward thinker in various areas, including strategy and interrogation. Carter Dixon exited his cabin numbered 35, grabbed his pistol, which he holstered, and grabbed a compound crossbow, which was a gift last year's Christmas to him.

"Hey, you fuckers get your lazy ass up; we have to go out and hunt before those fucking rotters come around to eating our food!" said Carter Dixon, still hollering like a common hillbilly; he heard his brother and sister mutter something as they got up and got dressed before grabbing their equipment. Once his siblings joined him outside, they both hopped onto their motorcycles and headed a little bit further south to hunt away from the group, but close enough to where they needed help, and they were within shouting distance. Carter hopped onto his sister's motorcycle and rode with her as they followed Atticus on his bike to wherever they would be hunting.

King

James County, Georgia

Marcus Wayne and Randall Welsch stepped out of their truck, and the two exited with their guns ready. Marcus and Randall were horrified at the scale of destruction that had been unleashed; Marcus held his Colt Python Magnum in his hands as he cocked the gun, putting a bullet into the chamber in case something came towards him. Randall moved with his shotgun as Marcus ran parallel with him; they were parked outside an old military checkpoint. Randall and Marcus were horrified to see so many bodies of people caught in the middle of the bombing, and the scene reminded Marcus of looking at crime scene photos.

"Jesus fucking Christ, man, these people, man." Randall was just as surprised as Marcus was at the scene unfolding before them; they were shot in the head or torn apart by the dead. Marcus stepped over a woman who was missing her lower half and was slowly decaying, but she was shot in the head; Marcus stopped as they heard a snarl and turned slowly to see a zombie get up. Randall and Marcus stepped back as they aimed their weapon.

"All right, man, you got the shot for the head."

"I want to ensure that this isn't a prank and that I am not doing something if this person is alive."

"He isn't alive, Marcus; takes the fucking shot." Said Randall as he heard Marcus's gunfire hitting the zombie in the head and killing him once again; he was wearing his old mechanic clothes. Marcus walked over to the body and kicked it, making sure it was dead; he searched the pockets of the dead mechanic and found his wallet, which he opened to look at the man's driver's license, which stated his name as George.

"His name was George; he was an organ and had a girlfriend." Said Marcus as he pulled out of the wallet a picture of George with his girlfriend at a restaurant. Randall nodded as he continued to scan the area; after that, the two of them headed deeper into the town to see more bodies mixed with soldiers, with the same scene playing out as if it was on a loop. Marcus and Randall entered a gun store shop, and inside it, the two searched the store, and once it was clear, they grabbed some over-the-counter duffel bags and loaded the bags with ammo and guns. Marcus placed the bags neatly, and they were hunting rifles, pistols, and automatic rifles. Marcus also placed the boxes of ammo into the bag and took what stock remained of the knives. The gun store looked to have been looted after everything or during everything that had transpired while he was in a coma. Marcus and Randall realized that the store with everything they were taking was the last of the stock; nobody, at least in this decade, would replenish the supplies. They continued deeper into the town, and they avoided the large clusters of the dead that were congregated around certain areas. Marcus and Randall stopped as they peered from the alley down a street to see three, maybe four, of the dead devouring a deer that wandered into the town. They could hear the dead snarl and moan as they ripped deeper into the deer; blood and guts were everywhere.

"It seems like these bastards are enjoying their morning breakfast; the one thing Marcus that you have to learn is that the dead aren't that dangerous when they are alone. But when they are in a group like that, they take longer to take down; by then, you would get tired and run out of ammo. I learned this because the military had reports or details on how to kill the dead if they approached people; I even overheard from the military how they killed some of them. Listen, we move quietly and quickly but not too quickly where we attract attention." Said Randall as he whispered to Marcus as they checked left and right to see if any more of the dead were coming; they occasionally looked behind them as well. Once they gathered enough information, they were clear to move to expect the other ones down the street eating a deer; they moved into the town's local family-owned grocery store.

Marcus and Randall searched the grocery store, which was looted and vandalized; they both saw signs of a struggle inside the building because of their roamers with bullet wounds to the head and empty shell cases. Marcus and Randall stepped over the bodies and saw that this was someone's last stand when things were going south; they had their weapons drawn, ready to be used as soon as they entered the store. The smell was horrible; it smelled of rotting flesh and gunpowder, and the smell of burning oil and buildings was powerful. They had their duffel bags slung over their shoulders and knew they would gather what they could before returning to the car with the supplies they had gathered over their run.

"Marcus, there is some bottled water; we could bring the car around here and place some clean water bottles into the flatbed." Said Randall after clearing his part of the building and noticing the bottled water on the racks ready to be sold. Marcus walked, hearing his name being called, and nodded at what Randall was saying.

"Why don't I grab the car and bring it to the front of the grocery store?" asked Marcus, who saw that Randall agreed and threw the keys to Marcus, who caught them; he exited the grocery store and headed towards the truck.

Meanwhile, Randall searched the rest of the building and killed a woman who once worked at the grocery store with his switchblade, and he stabbed the female zombie in the brain, killing her again. He gathered the supplies or what remained of the supplies near the front door of the building as he waited for Marcus to come back with the car.

Marcus Wayne used the alleyways and took cover behind trash cans or dumpsters; he avoided the dead wherever possible, saw the scale of destruction from the bombing, and stopped as he reached the car and heard the sound of a helicopter flying over or hovering in the sky. Marcus slowly looked up into the sky to see that the sun was shining fully in the morning sky, to see a helicopter that looked to be a military fly over and stop as if it was hovering. Marcus watched as the helicopter began to fly away and head in a direction that appeared to be heading north towards Atlanta or somewhere else. Marcus opened the driver's side door, put the keys to the ignition, and drove towards where Randall was in the grocery store. Marcus exited the truck and helped Randall gather the supplies; they stopped and listened as they heard the sounds of the dead approaching them. The two of them began to move faster, placing the duffel bags into truck and water and canned food; Randall found medicine inside the grocery store and placed that into the truck.

"Did you see that helicopter, Randall?" asked Marcus, hoping he wasn't going crazy.

"No, you are probably hallucinating, Marcus; it happens. Take some water, man; I'll drive to camp. We need to leave now, or there will be no-way-out Marcus." Said Randall as he took the keys from Marcus's hands and waited for his friend to hop into the truck. Randall drove out of their old town, which was very much in ruins, and hopefully, someone would rebuild the town in the future.

The two of them returned to camp and began to move their supplies into a cabin that would serve as the storage for everything. Not knowing he had blood from the zombie, he shot and didn't realize it; Marcus hugged his wife and son. Marcus had learned lessons that would prove valuable from his best friend, the man who had his back many times. As the morning turned to the afternoon, Marcus sat in the leather chair of the cabin and looked through his wife's scrapbook of old family photos as well as gatherings. He smiled at looking at the photo of his grandfather who had fought in the second world war and the Korean war, his name was Ian Wayne. He turned sharply as if his ears were straining to hear the sound of wooden floors creaking, he looked to see his wife was wearing her normal clothes. A short-sleeved shirt that was her exercise clothes as well as her yoga pants, he smiled seeing how beautiful she was in everything she wore.

"You're looking at the family scrapbook again, my love." Said Maggie as she smiled at him, knowing that everyone else at the camp was struggling to understand what was happening or what had happened.

"Yeah, I am, I stumbled on the picture of my grandfather Ian Wayne. I was just remembering something I asked him when I was a little kid."

"Yeah, what did you ask him?"

"I asked him, we were discussing what I was being taught in school about the Second World War and the Korean War, I asked him…how many Germans or Japanese did he kill during the war as well as how many Koreans did, he kill in the Korean War? He smiled and said I killed a lot in my life, hopefully, it's something that you don't do and you live a life that makes people feel uncomfortable with. He admitted that sounded crazy and it did at first but he said that when you have a group of people who count on you that's your brotherhood. "Said Marcus as he smiled remembering when he was just a young kid and being amazed by his grandfather's story.

"My love, in this world we have to be ready. I know everyone is losing track of the days and the weeks as this continues, you have to be ready like everyone else has to be ready. People will die and our group is your brotherhood. I feel like Randall will start to shatter with his leadership over the group, people will start looking to another person to lead the group. Randall and everyone are stressed because what has happened, our world is now the dead's and we have to claw our way slowly to the top again. Remember these words when I tell you. We survive or we die in this world, your family and your brotherhood this group has to see it till the end. I want you to be ready if I don't live through this, you have to be ready to teach Connor how to survive from the many lessons you are getting from Randall. You help people around the camp and they see you as person who could become the next leader, we have to be ready for anything my love. Because I need you to be ready if I don't live or something happens to me."

"I won't let that happen Maggie, I won't lose you. We have some supplies and we have rotational shifts for guard duty. We are far away from Atlanta and living in a campsite, Carter and his siblings are right now as we speak getting more food for us when winter arrives." Said Marcus as he wiped the tears from his wife's face and smiled at her with nothing but kindness in that smile, she smiled at him as well.

"You have nothing to worry about, we can get through this and we can claw our way back." Said Marcus repeating what she told him and smiled once again, somewhere in his heart he knew that people and a lot of the group weren't going to survive. But the very image still came into his mind of seeing the helicopter flying over his old town and hovering as if he locked eyes with the pilot, he knew what he saw and he wasn't crazy. Marcus kissed his wife on the lips as they passionately showed affection towards each other, his wife kissed him as she sat on his lap facing the window. The two as they kissed passionately took each other's clothes off and quickly fell into a series of events, Maggie smiled seductively seeing Marcus without his shirt on and they both began to make love with one another. Maggie Wayne moaned as Marcus slide his penis inside her and the two kissed one another, it had been a while since the two of them had sex. They didn't need to worry about Connor, he was at the local school and wouldn't be back for hours. Their small group had made the decision for a school to be opened inside one of the RV's so that the children would have a sense of normalcy even as the world had gone silent. Marcus and his wife continued to have sex on the chair as they moaned in pleasure as they felt their hips touch and the sweat was beginning to build as they continued to make love into the early evening, once they were finished, they placed fresh clothes on them and picked up Connor from school and gathered with everybody to eat dinner. Once dinner was finished the group went their separate ways and returned to their cabins to rest.

Randall Welsch took his shift to watch the perimeter of the campsite and sat on the roof of his cabin, but instead of watching the perimeter he had his binoculars pointed in the direction of his friend's cabin and was looking at his best friend's wife with nothing but lust. Randall even back in high school had a crush on Marcus's wife, he even when he dated his girlfriend before the world fell imagined her. He always kept his thoughts private, but he couldn't help himself. He saw himself the better man than Marcus, he could protect Maggie and Connor. He knew that Marcus wasn't going to survive this, he wasn't born for this and he certainly wasn't ready for what would come next in this insane world. His thoughts ran wild with not right away but getting rid of Marcus, maybe on supply run and saying that the dead got him and he watched his friend get torn apart. He wanted to embarrass Marcus about him seeing a helicopter, but he wanted to bind his time. He was already the leader of the group but he craved more and he wanted more than that. Randall stopped watching the house and watching as Maggie Wayne took off her clothes into her nightgown, he grinned as he watched that and turned away as soon as Marcus went into the bed.

"Marcus Wayne is a threat to my leadership of this group; I shouldn't have rescued him when everything was going wrong. I see how people around camp look to Marcus for advice or I see him help the people around the camp with issues that arise. He is threatening my position and I have to get rid of him somehow." Said Randall to himself and smiled at those words. He watched the camp throughout the evening and he rotated his shift for the next person. Randall in his mind was plotting what he would do to Marcus and either kill his friend or remove him from ever becoming the leader.

6

Chapter 4

Two

Months Later

Marcus Wayne woke up earlier than the others and walked over to find the park Ranger's vehicle, he grabbed the keys and turned the car over. He drove out of the camp and headed towards Atlanta, he wanted to check something and see if he was in fact going crazy. He was curious about the helicopter and he wondered if the military were still somehow operating. He turned on the lights as he drove down the dirt road, it was still dark and the sun was beginning to rise. He continued his drive and looked to his right as he saw in the car the radio that was common among law enforcement, he turned the radio on and he switched the dial to broadcast as he drove towards Atlanta.

"If anyone is listening to this, if anyone is still alive out there. This is Deputy Marcus Wayne from King James County Georgia, if anyone can hear my voice. We can get through this, all of us together. It's us against the dead, the living against the dead. I know it seems like we can't fight back and its our extinction event, but I believe in something greater. I believe in hope and I have seen throughout human history, when we are in life-or-death struggle. We can do amazing things if we band together and fight things, it doesn't have to be like that and we don't have to go back to the dark ages. I was in a coma when all this was going on, like I said I was an officer and I was shot on duty during an armed robbery call at a bank in my town. Whatever happens, whatever comes next. We will all win, we've already won. We survive or we die, it's that simple." Said Marcus afterwards he signed off, he hoped that someone heard his message and knew that they weren't the only survivors in the world.

It had been a few hours later, when Marcus arrived in the city of Atlanta. He exited the Park Ranger's patrol car that looked very much like his old police cruiser and placed the keys into his pocket. He was almost blown away by how much destruction had been wrought onto Atlanta, the buildings were a maze of fallen bricks and masonry every so often he would see rebar sticking out from the piles of rubble. As he walked further into the city he noticed the charred remains of people, they were put down and he didn't see them as a threat. He continued walking as his cowboy boots stepped onto the pavement and the concrete, crushing some pebbles under his foot. He had his hand hovering over his colt python magnum in case the dead wanted to eat him, he would defend himself. He knew that the dead roamed around in the city if they had a constant food supply, he had gone with Randall to recon the city and saw from a good distance within the city that the dead were all over the place. He was worried for Randall, he believed that their friendship was beginning to fall apart and that the stress over the months of being a leader was getting to him as well as the collapse of the world. He stopped as he heard the sound of the dead within a block or two, he froze as he recognized the sound of gunfire followed by a man saying that he was reloading. Marcus quickly began to jog where he was hearing the gunfire. He was happy and excited that there were people who were still alive, it meant hopefully they heard his message on the radio. As he approached the sounds of gunfire, he stopped as he heard a person or persons scream in pain. Marcus sprinted and stopped as he saw a body a woman who from the looks of the uniform, she was wearing an old police uniform. He walked but stopped short as he heard the dead ripping into the woman that they were beginning to eat, he suppressed himself from tearing up and crying. He moved away from the female officer who's being ripped open by the dead, He kept his hand hovering over his colt python and was ready to quickdraw if necessary. He noticed the dead were busy eating the woman, he could sneak past since they were distracted and he moved into the street which had the same path of destruction. The city of Atlanta belonged to the dead and it was made clear, he saw burnt out cars and other vehicles as well as bodies that must have been killed when things were beginning to fall apart. Marcus moved with precision as he avoided the dead that he saw that were clustered together, he knew from Randall's teachings that the dead would be attracted to loud noises such as gunfire or car alarms or even loud music. Marcus in his mind had a question that kept coming to mind was what was his brother and his sister doing, He hoped they were okay and they were surviving. He stopped as he froze for a minute to see the Center for Disease Control building sticking out a sore thumb in front of his face, he noticed that the fences had fallen and there were so much military supplies still laying around everywhere in the city. He walked past the security checkpoint keeping his gun ready as he turned left and right to see bodies that were put down, many of the signs of the bodies and the scale meant the National Guard or some form of the military made their last stand at this very building.

Marcus entered the CDC and saw that they had limited power, the lights were on a constant emergency glow and there was so much dried blood where the military fell back to another set of defensive positions. Marcus stepped on empty shell cases and discarded automatic rifles that were empty of bullets, he noticed discard combat knives that had ran dull and were no longer of use to those that defended their station to the last. He had seen crime scenes before but this was way different than any other scene, he noticed the military had established their own set of defensive positions where they had a 50. Caliber machine gun pointed in the direction of the front door. The main lobby entrance smelled of nothing but decaying flesh and the smell of blood still lingered in the area, the national guard looked to have prepared to entomb themselves inside the building in an effort to contain the dead from going anywhere else. Marcus noticed C4 charges that were placed on the supports but were never detonated, he moved through the defensive sand bag emplacements and security checkpoints as he headed downstairs to where the scientists worked on studying new diseases.

He walked downstairs but stopped as he returned to the main lobby to look for a flashlight in case the facility ran out of power and he didn't stumble around in the dark. He kept his senses alert after grabbing the flashlight, he walked down the stairs and turned checking his corners as he raised his weapon. He moved slow and took his time, he also had his knife underneath his right arm that was holding his colt python and his knife blade was pointing wherever he turned his body. The emergency lights still functioned but how long would that last until the power ran out completely, the government and the military turned off the lights as well as internet all over the United States as well as taking control of the food distribution to the safe zones that were under the protection of the military. He noticed that the military downstairs had struggled in their last stand, they had no defensive emplacements and they used the various labs to separate the dead as they moved throughout the facility. Marcus could only imagine the fear in the soldiers' eyes as they struggled against the tide of the dead, hearing the screams on the radio as the military fought all across the state and all over the country. He closed his eyes and could almost still hear the echoes of the screams and the sound gunfire, as well as the frantic military calls for air support or artillery support. He reopened his eyes and continued into past the first series of labs where scientists worked on diseases for further study as well as protecting the public from outbreaks, he entered a room that was almost as vast as auditorium the ones of ancient Greece or ancient Rome. He stopped noticing that on the screen in front of him was playing a video that appeared to have been muted, he walked over to a computer to see it was on that screen and they were working in synch. He unmuted the audio and listened to the video of a scientist or a doctor giving what Marcus thought as his last message to the world before whatever happened to him.

"There isn't enough time for me to give my name or my position within the Center for Disease Control, but I have information for whomever finds this video and to see what had happened here. If you hear the gunshots in the background, the military are making one last desperate last stand against the dead that have entered the city of Atlanta. I am one of my scientists who have been studying this disease and its many similar symptoms to other diseases, it is almost as if the diseases have shared some of their symptoms. The disease we have named TS1S1-20 is a variant to T1S1-19, they both have similar patterns but are extremely different. The main disease T1S1-19 is very aggressive and its variants are even more aggressive, the only way from what out research states is there some medications that slow the disease progress upon being bitten or scratched and coming into contact with bodily fluids of the person or persons infected. The disease upon death reactivates the Occipital lobe which controls movement as well as vision and also reactivates the brain stem, the portions of the brain that controls your memories that makes you who you are doesn't reactivate. We know from watching footage from the military and the Police that a significant wound to the brain either from a knife or a bullet will end the reanimated subject killing it once again. This disease from some of our scientific minds have come to many conclusions, the disease functions naturally and unnaturally as if it was made by a threat from a outside threat. The Government as we know is investigating and the evidence points to a accident by German, Russian, Chinese, Korean, Japanese, British, French, Italian, Swiss, Australians, Vietnamese and Canadian scientists in an effort to make cure for the main disease, they unintendedly created the variants that have been spotted in certain nations as well as some sightings here in the United States including the variant where the dead have created dens in which they sleep and have called them hives in terms of how they act. "said the CDC doctor on his recording as he showed videos and pictures from the military as well as police showing the dens that were created in caves or old animal dens, it was one of many instances that Marcus was beginning to feel terrified that the dead were able to create dens that looked almost like cavemen settlements. But many of the pictures he recognized were from United States military activities in Canada as well as Alaska from what he heard when he was in hospital, the video continued and the Doctor stopped speaking for a bit as a soldier came to him telling him he has less than two minutes because the dead had breached the outer fences of the CDC that he came through. The Doctor continued to explain other variants such as those that are able to run and climb as well as protectors that shield a horde from bullet fire in order to keep the horde safe, Marcus was horrified to hear about some of the other variants that the dead were able to use their stomach acid to kill a person or persons. The video ended with the Doctor leaving as some soldiers grabbed him and headed for the nearest exit, Marcus was shaking and he was terrified at everything he learned since he was in the hospital things were much worse as well as the last thing the doctor said we are all infected. Marcus walked away from the conference room or control center, he moved into another part of the building and saw a map that showed the United States of America as well as maps of CDC facilities, plus military safe zones that were mapped out. Marcus noticed a file that was left behind in the rush of the evacuation of contingency orders in case the safe zones fell. Marcus noticed that a page was missing from the many papers that were present, it meant that something was on that page that was meant to be kept a secret.

"What do you have to hide, why is a file missing within this folder?" asked Marcus to himself and thought it was odd that a file within a folder that listed orders from the military was missing, he noticed that this structure underground was once a lab and was converted into a temporary intelligence station for the military. He noticed radios, computers, maps and blueprints of construction from the military of various projects. Once Marcus was finished investigating the underground, he returned to the surface and exited the CDC that was now the sight of battle in which the military had lost. Marcus was curious as what that file had, he noticed it was full of contingency orders of fallback plans in case the infection got way too out of hand. Marcus headed back to his car and moved slowly as means to avoid detection.

Marcus was close to his car and killed a few of the dead with his knife, leaving behind corpses and his clothes had stains of blood but he didn't care. He was still in shock about everyone who was surviving, was infected with the disease the main one that appeared in 2009 with isolated sightings and reports. The city of Atlanta was filled with the dead, he was careful to avoid the major clusters of the dead and there were many of them that were all over the city. Marcus killed the dead that were isolated from the rest and made sure to use his knife rather than his gun, he knew from what Randall told him was the dead were attracted by loud noises. Marcus had a bad feeling that if the dead ran out of their food supply, they would move out from the city and head further out as they searched for food to consume. He just wished they were long gone before the dead ever left Atlanta and headed elsewhere. He took one last look of the city, and saw that some of the dead were slowly walking or were following him after leaving the CDC. They were slow and he had time, he entered into the old Ranger's patrol vehicle and drove away as the dead approached slowly by the time they reached where Marcus was, he was gone.

Marcus drove away from the city of Atlanta, the city was all but lost the dead now walked its streets. But he left learning more information than he could possibly have dreamed of, he understood a little bit of what had occurred and he knew that everyone who was living were infected that all it would take was you to die. Marcus returned to the campsite close to midafternoon and exited the car to see his family running to see him, he embraced them in a hug and smiled with joy hiding what he learned even though he was covered in the blood of the dead. Before Marcus walked away with his family he paused while he had everyone's attention, he looked around to see Randall as well as the other survivors.

"I went to the city of Atlanta by myself this morning, and I learned information that I have a better grasp of what occurred while I was in hospital. I went into the CDC and watched a video that was playing in a loop and I understand things better than I thought I would, I think we should be alarmed because I have troubling news this disease has related symptoms to anthrax, rabies, meningitis, the common flu and many other diseases that it shares symptoms with or have stolen the symptoms from the diseases I named. The video that was playing was a former doctor who worked at the CDC and it looked to have been on a loop before being sent or uploaded for future reference to the cloud, I listened to the video and learned that this disease on accident and naturally has variants of the same disease but have a completely different affect to those that are infected or have died. I also learned that we are all infected and all we have to do is just die, then we turn. Listen in this world I have learned only two things you survive or you die, I don't care if when we die become the very thing we are fighting because I refuse to just surrender! It's us against the dead and once this is all over, we have to choose to start life all over again bring order from the chaos! We are in a state of chaos, our world belongs to the dead and I want to change that because we aren't the dead! We tell ourselves... We tell ourselves we survive or we die!" said Marcus Wayne to see people's faces change from fear to courage as he spoke, he never knew he was a man of words or giving speeches. Suddenly to the left of Marcus's vision, Randall clapped his hands together mockingly.

"Well, isn't that the fucking speech of the year or wait, there isn't reporters here. I am the leader of this group Marcus; I make the calls not you! So, this is the new you, I saved your ass from that hospital and I protected your family until your whore of a wife wanted me to risk my ass to that hospital to save your coma induced self!" shouted Randall with rage, Maggie Wayne looked at Randall with disgust as well as feeling like she got punched in the gut. Marcus heard what Randall called his wife a whore and rushed Randall giving him a punch straight to his face, giving Randall a right hook. Everyone heard the punch connect and as well as hearing the sound bone breaking, Randall stumbled backwards as Marcus continued to throw punches at Randall as well as kicks, Randall took the blows as well as grunted in pain as he felt the full force of Marcus's blows. Marcus only felt rage and continued to defend his wife's honor as he beat the crap out of Randall, he grabbed Randall and flipped him over his shoulder as he placed his knee against Randall's neck. Randall struggled to get free and tried punching Marcus's knee but with no effect, Randall summoned his strength and managed to free from Marcus's pin and renewed his assault against his former friend. Marcus dodged as Randall threw punches, some managed to connect against Marcus with almost no effect. The fight ended when Marcus grabbed Randall's arm and did an armbar as he followed up with a knee to his former friend's face breaking his nose, before Randall could stumble away and cover his nose. Marcus kicked Randall's knee and a loud audible crack was heard as Randall's leg was broken. Marcus stepped back winning the fight against Randall as he saw his former friend, holding his knee and his nose as he moaned in pain after being both beaten in a fight as well as embarrassed. Marcus took slow deep breathes and was somewhat shaken even though he acted in self-defense, he never thought that he would have to fight his friend that nothing would happen in their friendship. Marcus was in the officer corps of the military before becoming a deputy, he had seen things and done things but the fight between them felt wrong. Marcus watched as two men who were survivors grabbed the Randall and brought him to his cabin where they would do first aid on his injuries, Marcus had his blood and the dead's blood as well as Randall's blood on his face plus his clothes. Marcus could tell that something was changing or had changed since the apocalypse with his friend Randall, he stood there watching Randall being carried to his cabin and his wife was trying to get his attention by placing her hands on his face as she wanted to look him in the eyes. Marcus snapped his attention to the present and looked at his wife Maggie Wayne, who was worried for Marcus and he turned his head to see that Connor was also somewhat scared as they both watched the violence that unfolded.

"I'm okay, Maggie. I'm okay." Said Marcus as he nodded as his head and kissed his wife who smiled at the relief of hearing his voice, Marcus walked over to his son and knelt the two embraced after a moment where Connor was afraid to hug his dad.

After the violence that unfolded between two friends who called themselves brothers, Marcus felt like he was changing as his thoughts and mind replayed the events. Marcus closed his eyes trying to push the events in the back of his mind or erasing what had occurred, but his mind was telling him that he was changing and that this world was causing his moral code to slowly erode. He was in the cabin; his wife and son were out forging for berries that were growing in the wild was well as mushrooms. He heard the sound of motorcycles and a truck that was arriving back at camp which meant that was the Dixons that were arriving, the Dixons from what he heard from people at camp had a long family history within Georgia that their ancestors settled in this state when there were only Indians walking around. He even heard that the Dixons, were involved in the Civil War that their forebearers served in the Confederacy and his family had a rich history of being in law enforcement, the military sometimes having family members that were criminals. Marcus stepped outside without his shirt and still had the blood of the dead and Randall's blood on his face, Carter walked over to him and thought that something happened while they were away but Marcus could tell that something was bothering them.

"What is it? It looks like you have seen a ghost while you were away, I see you and your family brought the camp food as well as some fresh water that needs to be cleaned before drinking in case the disease is water borne."

"Yeah, we have days if not weeks to leave this place. We drove by Atlanta and stopped, we noticed that some of the dead that were in the city have begun to move outwards. I think their food supply from deer that have wandered inside is running dry and the dead only follow sound as well as what they see, we need to start placing less wood in our campfires and as well as the lights somewhat deemed. We need to start training people on how to fire a gun and how to reload as well as gun safety. I don't want to cause panic, but I feel like it should be better that people are carrying a gun and know how to use it. But it looks like you've been through hell and I caught some bits of conversation that you went to Atlanta by yourself and went into the CDC to find a video of some doctor that was playing a loop that states we are all infected, I heard what Randall called your wife a whore. I got the feeling I would hate that son of a bitch." Said Carter with his southern accent, his voice sounded like gravel as he was a smoker, his brother Atticus was known in law enforcement for selling meth and other drugs and Carter had arrested his brother more than one occasion.

Marcus felt like things were changing fast and had to brace himself from not stumbling to a chair, it felt a wave had hit him that this is what life would be like for the foreseeable future. Carter and Marcus locked eyes with each other, as Carter saw the fear in Marcus's eyes which told him the truth that things were going to be getting much harder from here on out.

"I felt like you should know, because with you beating the shit out of that dickless motherfucker Randall. We are looking to your leadership; you can always count on me Marcus." Said Carter as he walked away after giving Marcus a report of the situation, Marcus stood there at the doorway leading into the cabin and watched as business went somewhat back to normal.

In the city of Atlanta, the dead roamed the streets and snarled as well as groaned to one another. The dead only roamed to feed and were beginning to leave the city of Atlanta as if they were migrating like birds or wild animals.

On the hill within the campsite, Marcus and Carter as night slowly drew near looked through Carter's night vision binoculars to see the city of Atlanta watching the dead who still looked human except for the open wounds that covered their bodies. They were far enough away and Marcus zoomed in with the binoculars to see that the dead were slowly moving away from the city, Marcus wondered if there were the variants that the CDC doctor on the video talked about were within this horde.

"It looks like we have days at most, worse case we might be looking at a week." Said Marcus as he looked at Carter who nodded his head thinking of the same thing.

"Okay, when do you think we should let the group know? This is a security issue and we need to let them know, because I just have suspicion that people are going to die and if you, we are right then that would mean that these people don't have the time for the training."

"Yeah, I agree. This is something we should let them know at the dinner, have someone bring Randall his food as well as place some cuffs on him. I am starting to feel that something is wrong with Randall that when this happened, he has changed from the man I once knew and the man I called my brother." Said Marcus as he placed his hands in front of him after handing Carter his binoculars, Carter nodded his head and took the binoculars as he walked down the hill with Marcus.

The survivors from King James County or what remained were gathered at the campfire as they ate the food that was hunted and the food that was forged by Maggie Wayne as well as her son Connor Wayne. Marcus sat with his wife and son as they ate the deer that Carter hunted, the atmosphere at the campfire was nothing but happiness and joy. However, Marcus and Carter as well as his siblings knew that they would have to tell everyone more bad news in the same day.

"I am sorry to interrupt everyone as they are eating but I have news, I know that earlier today I gave you the worst news that we are all infected and that there are variants, however Carter and I did some recon on the hill that has a perfect view of Atlanta at least the portions we could see. He informed that the dead were slowly leaving Atlanta because from what his siblings could interpret is they are running out of food within the city, like I said we went to the hill and used binoculars to see the city. Carter and his siblings are right, the dead are slowly leaving the city. So, I am letting everyone know that we are going to start training those that are old enough to learn how to use a gun as well as setting up defenses in case the dead stumbled upon our safe zone. I think that is also time for us to go on supply runs for guns and ammo, in order for us to maintain our equipment." Said Marcus as he saw everyone's faces turn from happiness and pure joy to a face that resembled, they were afraid but they wanted to fight as well. Marcus felt like he was an officer again and knew what leading was people as well as listening to those who would advise him, he hoped that these people would fight every inch but they weren't ready and needed to be trained as well as equipped. Marcus spent two years in the military, he was in the national guard of Georgia and was an officer and he was also at that point he was also a deputy in the sheriff station at the town he was born in.

Once the dinner was over, Marcus took first watch in the cabin as his wife and son were asleep. He looked from the window with his colt python holstered to his hip and his hand was on the butt of his revolver.

7

Chapter 5

Seventeen Miles away from Atlanta, Georgia

Three Weeks later

Marcus Wayne and some of the survivors were trained in hand-to-hand combat as well as in gun safety including how to use a gun. Carter and Marcus had kept their eyes on the city of Atlanta, they wouldn't have the ammo to deal with the dead. The two of them were planning for the departure of the campsite and leave for Savannah Georgia in which they would set up basecamp before going on the road again. They had a plan and told the rest that they would be leaving for Savannah Georgia where they could rest as well as gather their strength before leaving the state all together, Marcus outlined the plan that they would after going to Savannah Georgia leave for Saint Louis Missouri. Marcus walked to the cabin and began to pack his bags getting ready to leave, his former friend was free but was looked down upon by the group. Marcus would show mercy to those that were his former friends until they did something towards him again.

Marcus Wayne also packed Connor's bag and once that was finished, he walked out of the cabin as he headed for the parked vehicles that were being refueled as well as getting ready to scout the nearby roads. The group was around twenty to thirty-two survivors that either lived in King James County or joined the columns of survivors as they headed to the campsite where they were now. Marcus had met some of the survivors that were in his group, they looked to him for leadership and he took care of those that looked to him for guidance. The group were using the three RVs to transport the group that didn't arrive in vehicles, the third RV was slowly converted into a transport in which the supplies would be stored such as food, medical, ammo, guns and water. The distrust between Randall and Marcus was getting wider, the two of them in the public eye worked with each other and in the private they felt as if one another had their own civil war brewing. Marcus noticed that Carter Dixon and Martha Dixon sided with him as well as of course his wife as well as their son sided with him, he even a made a note that Atticus Dixon was siding with Randall and not many of the other survivors sided with Randall than they did with Marcus. Marcus Wayne, Maggie Wayne, Carter and Martha Dixon believed that there was a civil war brewing within the group and they knew that this would spilt the group apart until someone ended the civil war either from peaceful methods or violent methods. Marcus had killed people before but when the world was overrun by death, every person was alive mattered and that the dead were the threat now. Marcus had read comic books that had zombies in it and he remembered the quote they always used which was fight the dead and the fear living, but right now the only person he feared was his former best friend. He knew that if Randall forced his hand, he would have to kill him and that his friend knew some of his tactics but he didn't know the training he received when he was in the national guard and the army. He was taught in the national guard how to survive and to never give up, he was a brilliant strategist and was even better in terms of logistics. He was taught many things that he was trained to become, he was taught by his squad members that the importance of survival was to study your enemies and to see how they act before you strike. He walked and his cowboy boots crunched under his heel as he stepped on the gravel road, he took a deep breath feeling the fresh air fill his lungs with a sense of calm passed over him. He heard Carter and his sister approach him with some fireworks they found at a supply run earlier in the week, he knew what they were playing to do before they left to distract the dead.

"We are thinking about setting up these fireworks before we leave and setting them off as a way to distract the dead to buy us time, I have some teams right now who were former construction workers building some breastworks in which the dead could fall into them as a means to lessen their numbers. It could buy a lot of people time and it could give time for us to evacuate in an orderly fashion as well as meet at the agreed rendezvous point in which we will take I-75 to Macon before heading towards Savannah Georgia we will meet everybody at Macon, before we push into Savannah." Said Carter as he reiterated the plan to Marcus, except adding his own addition to the plan. Marcus nodded as he followed along and was thinking that it could work but it could also cause a panic, he knew that there their variants from the video he watched. Marcus agreed to the plan in theory, but in practice in would consider it and so he agreed halfway not completely because placing the fireworks would require them to enter the city and placing them at areas where the dead hadn't flood with their rotting bodies. It would also require somewhat to light the fuses and then rushing back to the campsite in order to leave with the rest of the group, but if there were the zombie variants nobody knew what to expect with them but Marcus only knew there was the variant in which the dead-built dens that acted as one that were like a hive mind or were coming back to life.

"What if we placed the fireworks around the city, maybe within the suburbs inside trash cans where there looked to be fewer of the dead around those areas. The dead follow noise and there aren't any more cars in the city so they could hear the sound to which they would follow, the dead aren't human anymore and they are nothing but monsters." Said Marcus and Carter nodded his head in agreement understanding the risks of going into the city as well as coming back out without having a guardian angel watching over you. Marcus, Carter Dixon and his sister Martha Dixon walked into a RV that was being fueled and would serve as the meeting room for the group's leadership to discuss plans or strategies. All three of them sat in the booth where the table sat in the middle of the booths and looked at one another, Marcus had things to get off his chest and he wanted them to know since meeting them that they were far more trustworthy to him.

"Listen, I know that some people are scared and that unease with the group is very much at a all time high. But I want to let you know that when I'm not around that you two will serve as my voice and will take matters into account if there is theft or a crime committed within the group, we need to hold onto our humanity because that is how we stay sane and survive this. I'm only in my early to mid-twenties and I have done a lot in my life being in the national guard at the age of eighteen, marrying my high school sweetheart becoming a father. I didn't take leadership of the group because I conspired to become a leader but rather because of other people's actions, power is a drug and it's an addiction like all those it corrupts the best and I fear that Randall was becoming corrupted by the whips of leadership. I don't take being a leader with pride or a badge of honor, I take it because

I have the wisdom as well as the foresight to keep these people safe. I trust you both to become my advisors, to be my naysayers and to be my in the chains of command if something happens to me that the two of you assume temporary leadership of the group. I need you both to promise me that if I die or something happens to me that you two take care of my family, to protect them as if they were your own." Said Marcus as he was making it clear that he was worried but he was making a promise from his inner most self that he would do anything to keep everyone safe and listen to their concerns or pleas. Carter and Martha Dixon nodded their heads seeing that Marcus was in fact a better leader as well as good man who wasn't drunk or becoming corrupted by power's temptations.

"We will protect your wife and your son, Marcus. I give our word to you that if anything were to happen to them, they would have to go through us." Said both Carter and Martha in unison, they both chuckled as well as Marcus seeing the siblings say exactly what the other was thinking. The three of them knew in their inner most thoughts that Randall was planning the same thing, Marcus for the first time in his life prayed to whomever would listen that he hoped the day would never come when he had to kill Randall in order to keep the group safe or the ones, he loved safe. Before Marcus say another word, they immediately stood up as they heard gunshots being fired from one of the cabins and the sounds of screaming as well as the all too familiar sound of the dead snarling. Marcus, Carter and Martha Dixon ran as they drew their sidearms sprinting out of the door to the RV to see some kids running as the dead maybe twenty of them roamed into their camp. Marcus fired a bullet from his colt python into the cranium of a zombie who was a woman wearing a waitress uniform, the zombie dropped onto the ground and was dead never rising again. Carter fired shots from his M9 pistol and reloaded when he was empty before firing again, Randall charged from his cabin firing his shotgun putting holes into the dead that came towards him. Marcus watched those that were trained to use guns fire their weapons into the dead aiming for the head which ended the reanimated corpses, Marcus watched as Martha used her two hunting knives to stab into the dead killing with the stab wound to the head or into the mouth. Marcus stopped and turned his head to the right to see a zombie in the distance running towards him like it was a cheetah, he sidestepped out of the way and did a wheel kick into the zombie's midsection stopping it in its tracks. He turned his weapon towards the zombie's head before blowing its brains out, Marcus was speechless that was in fact one of the variants and things were getting serious now. The small skirmish ended in the afternoon and the faces of those that weren't torn apart were covered with the blood of the dead, Marcus walked over to the body of an older man in his sixties who was being devoured by the dead when the skirmish first started. He holstered his colt python and pulled out his knife which was the knife he used when he was in the national guard, he stabbed the blade into the head of the man before he could turn. Marcus looked up to see that Randall was staring at him from a distance with the look of utter disgust as well as blaming him for what had occurred. Marcus, Carter and Martha as well as Maggie helped burn the bodies of the dead as far as they could from the camp. The rest of the group put down their fellow survivors who were torn apart and began to dig graves for them near a river in a clearing, Marcus lost only surprisingly ten people and knew that those ten people would forever be remembered even in death they would still be considered a member of the group.

Marcus dragged the zombie that ran towards him and the one he shot into the clearing by the small river, Carter and Martha Dixon were cutting down wood in which they were making stacks sort of like a funeral pyre where they placed the bodies of the dead on them after removing their wallets to see their names. The zombie that ran towards him like a cheetah was a convict, the man still wore his prison jumpsuit and he was no medical examiner but he could see that this man was bitten once on the hand before being shot from either a prison guard or another prisoner in the chest twice. They were wearing gardening gloves as they dragged the bodies to protect their pores from getting the blood of the dead, he saw Carter grab the legs of the convict and placed his body with care on the wooden pyre where Martha was placing some dried leaves onto the wooden stacks as well as on the bodies to burn them.

"I recognize this inmate; he was in at the Correction Facility where they kept the worst of the worst. I had to respond one time to a riot there, it was chaos. I remember the inmates when they were arrested telling us that some people had disappeared and were experimented on, I didn't believe it but there were strange things that some officers said that they saw and that the inmates that they arrested had needle marks in their arms as well as getting sick like the fever was like a furnace. "said Carter seeing the inmate who was laying on the wooden funeral pyre that they were strange needle marks on his arm as well as some areas where his body was reacted to something being injected into them, Marcus wondered if the government was indirectly experimenting on the disease before there was an outbreak.

"Do you think that the government or the military was experimenting with happened then on a smaller scale?"

"Yeah, it sure looks like the disease was both natural but also artificial in which someone made a mistake which costed a lot of people their lives and also that this person was running at you. I think the video you saw at the CDC was right and that the scientist was merely speaking out of mistakes that were made and that things exploded in their faces. Do you think that there is still a government out there and that they are planning to come back in an effort to correct the very thing that could have possibly made worse?"

"No, I don't but things are going to get more dangerous and that we have to prepare for every outcome in the event that things get worse." Said Marcus as he nodded to Martha after took their wallets before burning the bodies. The taking of the wallets was to find the IDs and to keep a historical account of what happened to the people who died in the collapse of society, Marcus knew that history would need an account of the lives that were taken and that in the centuries to come that people would study this to prevent another from happening. Marcus turned to see that Randall was approaching, he was angry and clearly looked to be causing trouble once again.

"So, the great Marcus Wayne, you failed this time as a leader and look at the people we lost. Hell, it would have never happened on my watch, those people would still be alive if we left already and headed to Louisiana. Listen man, you're a weak leader and maybe that coma did damage than it did from healing your wound or keeping you from feeling the pain of what happened to you in 2009." Said Randall blaming Marcus for what had occurred as Randall was talking to Marcus, Carter moved behind Randall keeping his gun behind his back ready in case things went south. Randall kept his shotgun in his hands knowing what Carter was trying to do and cocked his shotgun as he gave him a side glare, Marcus placed his right hand on his holstered Colt Python magnum's butt as if he was tempted to end this in the here and now before it happened in the future.

"Martha, go and tell everyone that we are leaving tomorrow morning at dawn for Savannah. Randall we can discuss this later and you as well as Atticus can go scout out the rest of the territory before we arrive at Savannah to find a location in which we can settle for the bit before making our way to the final destination." Said Marcus as he deescalated the situation that was unfolding before him and hopefully, he gives them an enough distraction in order to move towards the ultimate goal of surviving, it had been months since they hadn't spotted the military except for when Marcus spotted the helicopter and was dismissed by Randall. Marcus stared at Randall as the two of them locked eyes, before Randall walked away realizing this wasn't the time or the place, they lost half of their original group and it was time to move away from Atlanta.

Marcus and Martha walked away after several minutes, the two of them helped Marcus's wife and son to gather their stuff that was already packed. The survivors from King James County moved in a somewhat organized fashion and heard the sound of a engine revving as both Randall Welsch and Atticus Dixon drove away scouting the road ahead, Marcus breathed a sigh of relief and was the last man to get into the old park ranger patrol car and drove behind the third RV as Carter followed beside Marcus in his truck where on his flatbed was his motorcycle that had a tarp over it.

Randall and Atticus drove quickly as they scouted out the road ahead, they only stopped as they left behind bodies of the dead as they roamed around the empty houses or along roads. Randall was still fuming over what happened, it was all Marcus's fault and he should have stayed the leader but he would bide his time before taking back his old seat. He even admitted to himself that the horrors of this new world had begun to corrupt him as well as change him into something he wasn't recognizing as himself. Randall reloaded his Glock saw a zombie with both his legs shot to pieces crawling towards his boot, wherein placed his left boot against the head of the zombie and put two bullets from his Glock into the head of the zombie killing it. He turned to his right to see Atticus use the butt of his crossbow against the face of a female zombie before stabbing his knife into her skull, they were getting good at killing the dead and it was beginning to feel like a stress reliever as well as an exercise.

"Clear on my side, how about yours?"

"Yeah, it's clear, so I heard from Carter you were a cop with Marcus."

"Yeah, I was, that was a long time ago and you were nothing but a criminal before."

"Hell, I wore as a badge of honor because I felt like I was helping people and keeping people safe. I didn't abide by the laws of this country and wait this country doesn't exist anymore." Said Atticus as he gave a belly laugh and walked over to another zombie that was already approaching him and moved with speed as he brought the zombie's arm as he followed it up with a knife stab to the back of her skull, Randall rolled his eyes as he was just showing off his new found skills at killing the dead. Randall noticed lots of empty fields and some were empty farmland, he wondered if there were any good supplies left behind from people who were leaving from their homes or towns as the dead roamed the land. Randall knew that from what Marcus told him the city of Atlanta had about 4 million zombies, he could see why Marcus was sticking to the shadows as well as avoiding to fight, they didn't have the numbers for a fight a like that and even if they did, they would run of bullets before they reached the end of the horde. The dead were all over place and he could only guess how many were in

Russia there were probably a small band of survivors against millions of zombies. He chuckled to himself as he thought about turning on the news to see how the rest of the world was doing but he knew the cameras stopped recording a long time ago. Once Randall and Atticus checked the area for more the dead, they returned to their vehicles and parked next to the gas station as they refueled as well as gathering what supplies they could before continue on their way.

In the distance the convoy of survivors drove seeing the mess that was left behind by Randall Welsch and Atticus Dixon, the two of them, and in Marcus's inner most confines of his mind were preparing himself to fight for his family as well as those who now look to him for leadership. The convoy stopped once or twice to allow people to use the restroom and allow themselves to stretch their legs if they needed to, behind them it appeared that storm clouds were approaching and that meant thunderstorms. Marcus, Carter and Martha Dixon as well as the other survivors who were armed with guns waited for the rest of the survivors to finish what they were doing before continuing the journey towards Savannah. Marcus made a hang signal and word spread that it was time to keep it moving, they were wasting daylight as well as bad weather was approaching. The convoy rumbled slowly as they moved in a tight formation, the roar of the motorcycles echoed that seemed to be without end and the roar of the engines continued as they kept a moderate speed. Marcus smiled to himself thinking it was like back in the days when he was in the national guard and it was running with organization as well as efficiency. He felt even more happy with his family with him and they meant everything to him as well as the group of survivors that he was with that they were becoming his extended family.

The convoy regrouped with Randall and Atticus within Macon Georgia before steamrolling down into Savannah Georgia, they were stunned to see the damage wrought upon the city of the Macon Georgia as the buildings were either damaged or were completely destroyed. Parents adverted the eyes of their children away from the massive scale of destruction and seeing some of the dead were roaming the streets but were being put down by Carter. Marcus exited his vehicle and walked over to Carter Dixon after he killed some of the dead as well as leaving behind the carnage he conducted. Marcus turned his head to the right to see that Randall and Atticus were in their own circle as they looked at Marcus with some distrust, He turned his head as he made it clear that he was armed and placed his hand to the butt of his colt python magnum revolver. Carter finished off a roamer which looked to be a kid in his pajamas who died with a bite wound to the neck, Marcus felt sorry for the kid but also knew that he would be remembered in history as the countless people who died and turned.

"Yeah, what's up you ready to move out?"

"No, I think we are getting some bad weather soon and we need a place where we could hold out until tomorrow morning. I was thinking that we take the motel and clear it out to house our people and then we take the building behind me that fire station where we could house the rest, we need some areas in the motel that could be used as guard stations and another thing we could maneuver our RVs to block the road."

"Yeah, sounds good, do you want me to take first watch tonight or somebody else?"

"Yeah, take first watch and I know you are good with ranged weaponry such as the crossbow you use, I want your eyes perched on the higher ground to provide overwatch. I want Martha to take a secondary position over in the motel and your brother Atticus I want him to take Randall to scout out to find if there any radios we could use to maintain communication."

"Copy that." Said Carter Dixon as he walked over passing the orders to everyone on what their jobs would be for tonight's first pit stop, Marcus walked with his wife and son to a building with some other survivors to be their shelter for the evening. The RVs moved into their positions to blockade the road into town as the road out of town, some of the other survivors moved other vehicles into the small portion of town they were using for shelter. Marcus Wayne helped his wife get settled in the hotel's bed, in the bed was Connor Wayne who was already fast asleep and Marcus placed a chair as well as a table for him to use it as a stand for the sniper rifle, he brought with him. Marcus unzipped the duffel bag and pulled out the sniper rifle which was a Remington 700 sniper rifle, he kicked out the legs of the bipod and sat on the chair as he finished setting up the rifle to watch the street beyond where they could hopefully see any threats. He looked through the scope of the rifle and zoomed in as well as out, he was like a bird of prey watching for any threats. He knew that Randall would be hopefully returning with some radios that would make communication even easier, He saw a zombie that was walking around as he felt raindrops hit his head. Marcus smiled to himself and knew the rain wouldn't affect him, he was in his element and he was top of his class in sniping in the military. He waited had his rifle through the scope aimed at the head of the zombie that was once a doctor, he was still wearing his lab coat that had dried blood on it next to the open wound on his neck. He steadied his breathing and when he was ready once the wind was right, he held his breath and fired the bullet that with a high rate of speed penetrated the zombie's head killing it once again. He moved the bolt upwards and then downwards as the bullet that was used was ejected from the weapon, Marcus conducted the ritual again as he loaded a bullet into the chamber as he scanned the streets for anymore of the dead before sighting another one in which he fired again when the moment was right. As he repeated his ritual, he only stopped when he reloaded the rifle and he stopped firing once he saw Randall return with two duffel bags that were full of handheld radios from the police station as well as batteries that could be recharged. Marcus went to sleep once his wife Maggie Wayne took watch as she sat on the chair with her pistol on her lap.

Randall Welsch walked the street as he heard gunshots from Carter's vantage point, he walked from one end to the other as he held his shotgun. The storm above them raged and some of those that were on first watch were lighting some fires inside old businesses that had their windows smashed to all hell, it was getting colder and it meant that winter was coming. He walked over into the alleyway of two buildings and saw a fence where he walked past, he heard zombie growling at him as if it was a wild animal. He aimed through his iron sights of his shotgun and fired a shell into the zombie's skull which when the bloody mist cleared was caved in, He walked over and saw another zombie approach him coming towards the front like the other did. He killed that zombie without any remorse, he only paused as he walked over to see that the second zombie, he killed was a member of Macon's police. He took a deep breath and breathed out as if he was disappointed in himself for killing a fellow officer. He shook his head and cleared his mind as he told himself that this zombie was once a person but he had died, He knelt beside the body as he began to pant down the body for anything that might be useful. He stopped as he grabbed the gun from his holster as he checked the chamber to see if there were bullets inside, but he found it was empty. Randall threw the gun in frustration and walked away from the two zombies, he killed as he wanted to get out of the rain and get himself warm.

Carter Dixon went inside as he used the window to look at the street that laid beyond them, he saw some of the survivors were passing out radios that Randall found. He looked to his right to see that Marcus was awake and switched with his wife again, the two nodded at each other as the rain continued and Carter closed his eyes calming his body. Carter Dixon was an excellent hunter; he was excellent in the Atlanta Swat and he was an expert hand to hand combatant. He had training in boxing and even had some experience in martial arts, his sister Martha had the same experience and their family had a history that if the city of Atlanta. However, that never excused what happened to them in their childhood. Carter and Martha Dixon were both victims of abuse from their uncle who was known racist in the town they grew up, he was known for beating his wife and his brother's kids Carter, Martha and Atticus Dixon. Carter and Martha got the worse of the abuse rather than Atticus who was verbally abused, however his sister and brother were beaten almost daily. Carter and his sister Martha blamed the abuse that was caused on them to place Atticus onto the path of being criminal, they also blamed the rest of their family for not helping them. Carter was a teenager when his mom and dad told him that their uncle was murdered. It didn't faze him, he felt like some justice was carried out and his soul began to heal. He stopped thinking on the past and continued to finish his shift, before he took a moment to rest.

8

Chapter 6

Two Weeks Later

Savannah, Georgia

Marcus Wayne walked out of the room his family was occupying in the historic district of Savannah Georgia, it had been two weeks since they had left the campsite near Atlanta. He still felt exhausted and knew that his family was now safe for the time being unless something occurred, when they arrived at the outskirts of the city of Savannah it was deserted and they only saw the dead when they were clearing out buildings or in hotels. Marcus and the survivors of King James County began to think that the dead had begun to leave the bigger cities and were just roaming around, he walked through the hotel's hallways as he approached the stairwell that led into the lobby. He took a deep breath as he was walking downstairs and saw that the remaining survivors that weren't killed back in Atlanta were working hard, he heard Carter and Randall's voice as they were training some of the survivors how to shoot as they were firing at targets, they had setup. He walked down the stairs as his cowboy clumped on the wooden stairs and then thumped on the marble floor, he could already smell the fresh air and smiled to himself was once again. He knew his wife was regretting his decision about teaching Connor how to shoot, he heard his wife telling him that it could change their son into something it isn't supposed to be. His reply was that the world was already dangerous and he needed to know how to defend himself against threats, his son turned five and he needed to learn some ways to defend himself if need be. He stopped in the lobby and turned to see Martha was sharpening one of her knives as well as cleaning them, she was losing count of the dead she had killed and everyone else was getting better at killing them.

"Morning Marcus, how was your rest?"

"It was nice and it was good to get some peaceful sleep after our road trip, what has happened while I was asleep?"

"Nothing too crazy Marcus, we found some survivors held up in the river front. Atticus has taken over in helping the gun safety training and Carter has begun to interview the survivors we located. You would like to hear that two of the survivors we picked up were doctors in the local hospital, husband and wife."

"What were the other occupations of the survivors you found over in the river front?"

"One was a priest of the local catholic church; the others are rather a mix of occupations. There are two siblings who are both farmers who have been in Savannah since the beginning and they know some areas where we could find some good crop seeds."

"Interesting, did Carter discover how long they have been in Savannah or what they remember last before everything stopped?"

"Yeah, he is asking them now, he is interviewing them at the old police station and I'm sure he wouldn't mind someone else in the room."

"Yeah, I'll head up there and I have my radio clipped to my waist. If something comes up contact me and I'll be right there." Said Marcus as he patted the radio on his waist and saw Martha nod her head in agreement, he walked out of the lobby and headed towards the police station.

Marcus opened the front door of the police station and entered inside to be met by two sentries who were standing guard in the building, the outside of the building was made of brick and stone but the interior was half ancient as well as half modern. Marcus walked past the sentries and turned through a variety of hallways to a room that was labeled as the interrogation room, he opened the door to see Carter was about to jump to his seat but noticed it was Marcus entering the room. He nodded at Carter he sat down and took a seat next to Carter as he continued asking questions to a heavyset African American man.

"This is our group's leader Marcus Wayne; I hope you don't mind him entering the room."

"Not at all sir, nice to meet you, Marcus. As to your question Mr. Dixon, I was a surgeon and my wife was psychiatrist. My brother Marvin was in the FBI and I haven't heard from him in sometime. The last thing I remember was myself operating on a patient and then one of my nurses told me that we were evacuating. After that it was a blur until I remember the group that you are interviewing now, we've been held up in the river front for a longtime."

"May I ask your name?" said Marcus and the man who was a doctor looked at him as if he was surprised that he hadn't heard his name yet.

"My name is Frederick; my wife's name is Rose." Said Frederick who looked at Marcus who nodded his head. Frederick got up from the chair and saw Marcus offer his hand as the two shook hands.

"Welcome to the survivors, Frederick. You and your wife are in safe hands, it is going to take all of us to get this world back to what it was." Said Marcus as Frederick smiled, Carter also got up as he opened the door to where the detectives interviewed people. Marcus escorted the two doctors out of the police station and into the city of Savannah, the survivors were busy within their own territory which was the historical district and the river front district. The three of them walked past members of Marcus's group who were on patrol as they carried their weapon close to them.

"So, what did you do before this Marcus?"

"I was once a sheriff deputy in King James County, I was shot on duty with my partner Randall Welsch. It was a bank robbery call and when things got bad the doctors woke up from my coma where I saw Randall who took me to my family."

"That was a brave thing to do Marcus, Thank you for your service as an officer of the law."

"Well thank you for your service and your continued service as a doctor within our group. If you have any concerns or questions you can speak to me or Carter." Said Marcus as he stopped at the front of the hotel and saw Martha Dixon walk from where she was sitting to help get the new members of the group settled into their rooms in the hotel. Marcus nodded his thanks to Martha as she led the two doctors to their quarters in the hotel room, he paused for a moment as he looked out towards the sea and saw some members of his group using a boat, they found to gather food from the sea. He smiled and thought in his mind that it was important that in times when the world was full of darkness that it was important to find periods of light, he took a deep breath and felt his body feel with the warmth of the sun as well as his lungs feel refreshed from the clean air. After he took a moment to allow his mind to feel peace, he walked away from the sea view and walked to explore more the city.

Marcus left where his group had made a temporary home and entered the city that was still left unexplored, he watched his back as he moved beyond the perimeter of where his group called home. He noticed that the further he went into the city, the more damage he saw from vandals or destruction of property during the riots. He was alone in the city and his boots thumped against the cobblestone. He kept his hand on the butt of his revolver as he scanned the area in front of him for any threats, he was beginning to grow a beard and his wife didn't approve of his beard which made him laugh at some points whenever they discussed him shaving it. Marcus stopped in the middle of the street, to his right and left were store windows that were smashed in as well as some overturned bicycles. He kept his eyes forward and waited until he heard the sound again for him to draw either his knife or his gun, however he didn't hear the sound he thought. He couldn't help but think that he was being watched and if there were more survivors in the city that he didn't know about or was it just him going crazy. He stopped again as heard what he thought was someone coughing, his eyes went back to scanning the area around him like he was the terminator.

"My name is Marcus Wayne; I am sheriff deputy from King James County. I am the leader of the group that has come here to settle down before we make our trip to Saint Louis. I mean you no harm or any ill will, we have food and supplies as well as shelter if you need it. I heard one of you cough and if you need help, we have a doctor." Said Marcus however before he was going to continue his sentence Marcus took cover behind an overturned car as he heard gunshot that landed where he stood only moments ago. Marcus drew his revolver and waited as he heard two people wearing boots approach where he had taken cover. He heard their voices; he marked them as one being a female and the other a male. He waited as they got closer before he grabbed a hooded figure, who was heavyset and was armed with a double barrel shotgun. He grabbed the hooded male figure and disarmed his weapon as placed the barrel of revolver to his head, he also used his left arm around the man's neck.

"Drop your weapon!" ordered Marcus to the female who was stunned to see that someone got the jump on them, he watched as the hooded woman who was in her early twenties froze in either fear or in surprise.

"Drop your weapon, or he dies." Said Marcus as he added more pressure to his rear chokehold which caused the hooded male figure to choke as well as struggled to remove Marcus's arm from his neck. He stood there with the woman's partner or whoever he was to her, he looked at her with the same angry glare he gave to those he killed in self defense in war. He watched as the woman slowly dropped her hunting rifle to the street and then kicking it aside, he kept his eye on her as removed his grip on the man and stepped back aiming his revolver at them. The man coughed and struggled for air, the woman knelt in front of him and helped his breathing by keeping him calm.

"What do you want from us?" asked the woman to Marcus who stayed silent for a moment before speaking, he kept his gun raised and his finger next to the trigger.

"Nothing, as I said I am here with my people and we are settling her for a moment for the winter before leaving for in Spring for Saint

Louis. I am not here to kill or steal things from you, but you shot at me and I acted in self-defense."

"You almost broke my arm fucker!" shouted the man who had gathered himself and spoke as his arm was hurting, Marcus didn't move an inch and just looked at the man who was almost to tears. He realized that the man was also in his late or early twenties, he looked at them and weighing his options in his mind on what to do.

"You attacked me and shot at my feet, as I said before I defended myself. You were the threat and you were disarmed, I don't kill someone unless I'm forced to and you didn't force my hand."

"So, you disarm his weapon and almost break his arm." Said the woman who was believing that Marcus was going to kill them in cold blood, Marcus nodded knowing he didn't do anything wrong. He kept his weapon raised and heard a motorcycle driving from where his group were living, he heard the motorcycle stop to see Carter Dixon get off the bike and walk over keeping his crossbow raised at the two people who attacked Marcus.

"I heard a gunshot, hell we all did. I came over here thinking it was survivors warning us of a herd or something. But it looks like I found what happened here."

"Yeah, these two ambushed me, not successfully as you can see." Said Marcus as he pointed with his gun at the two figures who were at his mercy. Marcus watched as Carter was wearing the same clothes, he wore even more recently which was his motorcycle's club colors, Carter watched as Marcus restrained the man who fired his shotgun at his feet earlier ago. Marcus sat the man onto the curbside outside of a seafood restaurant, he then watched as Carter used his last handcuff to restrain the woman who was fighting back and it caused her to be slammed hard onto the cobblestone street which caused the her to go unconscious. Marcus stopped the man from getting up as he did what he was trained to do as an officer and threw him to the ground and placed his right knee into his back.

"Let go of me you son of a bitch! I'll fucking kill you and your entire group!"

"Shut the fuck up asshole, stop moving right now!" shouted Marcus again at the man as he squirming and trying to get out of Marcus's pin, Carter unclipped the radio and contacted for more backup which was responded by the distant sound of two motorcycles heading where they were located.

The two people who ambushed Marcus were brought back to where the survivors were located and were blindfolded to where they were placed in the old police station jail. Marcus watched as Carter removed the blindfold from the man who tried to get up but had his arm shackled to the bed in his cell, he watched as he struggled to get free from the handcuff but failed every minute and began to throw a tantrum like he was a child.

"Shut the fuck up!" shouted Carter as he slammed his crossbow's butt into the cell's metal door which caused the man to stop screaming for a moment, Marcus was already standing outside the other holding cell and opened it where the woman was located. He also removed her blindfold and found she was cuffed to the bed, she tried to use her legs to kick Marcus but never reached him. Marcus exited the cell and locked it with the keys he found that were in the drawer of what he believed to be the officer in charge of the station, he walked over in the hallway with Carter and discussed what their next move would be.

"Listen, I don't trust these people and something seems suspicious with them. I want you and your brother to interrogate them, they fired the first shot. I want to finish this and find out who they are as well as who they are with." Said Marcus and watched as Carter nodded his head in agreement, he watched as Marcus left the police station and went outside before he unclipped the radio.

"Atticus are you there? "Asked Carter as he waited a reply from his brother.

"Yeah, I'm here bro, what's going on?"

"I need your help with two survivors that Marcus encountered while on patrol, they fired on him and they are in the holding cells here at the police station. Marcus is fine, listen I understand we are having a disagreement but I need your help on this."

"Yeah, copy that bro, I'm on my way and is our beloved sis there."

"No. I'll contact her after you or if she is listening come meet us at the police station. Over and out." Said Carter as he switched the radio off and placed his sidearm as well as crossbow to a desk, he kept his knife in its sheathe as he waited for his two siblings to arrive.

It felt like hours when it was only fourteen minutes when Atticus and Martha Dixon arrived at the police station to see their beloved brother was sitting down in a swivel chair with his feet on a desk.

"Well, it looks like you guys are here. Let's get to work, Martha you take the female and your two brothers will deal with the man." said Carter as his sister give a brief acknowledgment before using a back up set of keys to unlock the door. Carter entered the cell first and uncuffed the man from his bed before dragging him to an interrogation room, Atticus was already there and had turned off the lights as his brother Carter threw the man inside thinking nobody was inside. The man stood up and saw nothing but pitch-black darkness, he saw underneath the door was the lights from the hallway outside.

"You think you are going to scare me, try something different." Said the man who didn't notice that someone else was in the room with him. Atticus watched the man in the shadows and blended in with his surroundings before he began to mouth breath, he saw the man jump and look around terrified.

"Where are you?!" said the man as he waved his arms around him trying to use his senses in order to get a feel of the room.

Carter stood outside the door before turning off the lights in the hallway and entering the room, he was accustomed to the darkness and had done raids in the dark. Both Carter and Atticus attacked the man who stumbled backwards into a chair from a powerful blow directed at him to his front. However, before he could counter what was done to him, he lost conscious and woke up to see that he was shackled to the chair.

"What's your name dipshit?"

"I don't fucking talk to you assholes, my people don't want problems with you."

"Until you ambushed one of us and you got your ass kicked." Said Carter and kept his eye focused as Atticus was behind the man in his chair as he put his finger in his mouth and slipped into the prisoner's ear who yelped in pain. Carter knelt so he could the man's face as he still in pain as he closed his eyes, he waited patiently for a minute before speaking.

"So, where is your group? How many people are in your group?" asked Carter and waited for the man to respond but no response came before kicked the folding chair down onto the concrete floor as his brother placed a washcloth over the man's face and handed Carter a jug of water where we began to pour on the man's face. The two brothers conducted to waterboard the prisoner who tried to move his head to get air, but began to choke and cough hard.

"Tell us where your group is motherfucker!" shouted Atticus to the prisoner who was still choking from the water going down his mouth and nose, once the prisoner stopped choking did, he speak.

"My name is Aiden and the woman in the cell her name is Courtney. We are with a group that outside of town on a farm, we went here to scavenge. We killed the group that lived on the farm and our leader used the people they killed as markers." Said Aiden as he struggled to breathe and knew that the torture wouldn't end because he revealed things about his group.

"What's your group name?"

"We don't have a name; we are just a group that formed when things collapsed and we went to some other communities where we raided them as well as raped the women. Courtney will know more, please don't hurt me anymore." Said Aiden as he began to cry as everything hurt and his body cried out in protest, he yelped in pain as Atticus grabbed a fistful of hair from Aiden who continued with the torture after Carter got the information he needed and exited the interrogation room to find Marcus.

Atticus continued to torture Aiden to gain more answers from him about the size of his group of raiders as well as the members in the group.

"I want to know exactly how many people you have Aiden." Said Atticus as he threw a heavy right hook to Aiden's jaw who shook with the force of the heavy right hook. Aiden turned his side to the left and spat blood out, he was in pain and he was getting hungry. He just wanted to go home and he wanted to sleep.

"Please stop, there are fourteen of us in our group. The leader's name is Matthew and the second in command is named Luke." Said

Aiden who was getting tired and knew he was close to blacking out, Atticus could tell that he was had enough and took the restraints off as he moved Aiden back to his cell where he shackled him to the bed.

"You will be fed soon and I will send a doctor in to treat your wounds." Said Atticus as he closed the cell door and locked it, as he walked to grab his equipment did, he hears his sister exit Courtney's cell. She walked up beside her brother who had knuckles that were bleeding, but knew he would handle it and probably go see the new doctor. Martha wasn't surprised that people were surviving still and that they weren't the only ones that were surviving.

"Did you get some intel from your friend?"

"Yeah, there's fourteen of them and his name is Aiden. The leader of the group is Matthew and their second in command is Luke, they are nothing but a group of raiders that have attacked survivor communities as well as killing them and raping the women. I'll talk to Marcus about it and see what he wants to do as well as talk to Carter since he oversees security, who knows we may go to war and crush them before they realize that their two friends haven't checked in."

"Yeah, but if they have fourteen people in their group and we've been recruiting people into our group our numbers should be sufficient. We are battle hardened against the dead at least some of us are battle hardened."

"Yeah, but we still have these new people that haven't been trained to use a gun or anything hand to hand combat related." Said Atticus as he finished placing his sidearm into his holster as well slinging his primary weapon over his shoulder before walking out leaving Martha behind who was grabbing her weapons.

Marcus Wayne and Carter Dixon listened to Atticus as well as Martha's interrogation of the separate prisoners, the two were listening with great interest. They met within the old hotel manager's office and the door was closed for complete privacy of the matter being discussed.

"So, you're telling me that these people have killed people and raped the women before either killing them or torturing them. Aiden told you that his group have only fourteen members and have set up shop in a farming community."

"Yeah, that's what he told me, we need to act fast and they may be wondering where their friends are if they haven't checked in for some time."

"True, however the new recruits aren't trained yet with hand-to-hand combat or firearm training. We won't be battle ready for six or seven weeks at the most, we could use one of the other hotels as a training ground for clearing out rooms as well as close quarters combat. If there is to be a war or we act in self defense against these barbarians, these murders and rapist, then we need to be ready and prepared." Said Carter as he laid out a tourist map of Savannah Georgia, it had many marks on it to represent where their group was located as well as where they had encountered other survivors who had joined the group. Those that Marcus and his group encountered within the city spoke of the same thing, that the city held on for three days and one week before falling. The national guard ordered civilians into their homes or businesses and lock the doors before either leading the dead away or sacrificing themselves by making a last stand further away from the city, this fact of encountering survivors inside Savannah had changed people's mind of that they were the last ones on earth. Marcus had however believed that there were more people out there because, he saw when he was the learner in this insane world a helicopter hover

over a building in his home town before flying away. Marcus studied the map and grabbed a map of Georgia as they marked the farm that was close to Savannah where the raiders were located. Marcus knew that if they were to strike them, they would have to cross deeper into Savannah as well as some other towns which could have threats hiding in any corner.

However, the members in this meeting that had experience were all present and were adding their own advice when needed, they all knew that winter was soon approaching and if they were going to be attacked it would be sooner rather than later.

Randall Welsch listened with everyone and a thought went into his mind of taking Atticus with him as well as some other people with the two prisoners to where the group was located. Randall knew that Marcus didn't have the stomach to kill them and it was an opportunity for him to show that he was the true leader of the group.

"I have an idea, one that could provide results for both opposing groups. Why don't I take some men with me as well as the prisoners to tell them, they could either leave or we could defend ourselves." Said Randall as everyone looked at him, Marcus shook his head and he knew it would be too risky. They needed more information and they needed to prepare themselves, if they rushed in it would be suicide and there would be causalities. They needed more information and they needed to prepare themselves, if they rushed in it would be suicide and there would be causalities. The meeting continued and there were arguments that broke out, the meeting only stopped when they thought they had enough of the argument and needed to work on the plan of training the newest members of the group.

Marcus was the last to leave and followed both Carter as well as Martha to the abandoned hotel that would serve as a training site for the newest members of the community. Marcus entered the building to see that it was a mess of luggage that was abandoned possibly during the rush of evacuations as the city was being defended by the military.

"Has this building been cleared out Carter?"

"Yeah, there were some dead here but not a lot. They were taken care of and thrown into the sea where I guess the fish are eating them." Said Carter as pointed his head in the direction of the sea that laid right in front of them. Marcus nodded and knew that fish needed to eat, he walked through the hotel as his two most trusted lieutenants walked behind him as if they were bodyguards. Carter turned on the flashlight and shined the light as they looked around to see the mess of papers that were all over the floor, there was dried blood in some areas where people were either bitten by the dead or were torn apart. Marcus had seen things in combat as well as a deputy and knew that the areas that dried blood was either a struggle or where someone didn't last long. Marcus stopped and knelt as he looked through the doorway of the manager's office to see dried blood that started at the door leading into the office where it looked that the manger fought until he died. Marcus walked into the office and saw two bodies of the dead that were put down by what he guessed was the manager who was trying to stay alive, he fought hard and he found the body of the manager who killed himself with a gunshot to the head. Carter and Martha sighed to see the body of the manger who was decaying, Marcus had seen crime scenes and death before it didn't faze him.

The three of them continued to walkthrough the hotel and saw bullet holes on the walls as well as dried blood that showed the national guard was here, the three of them saw the remains of what appeared to be the national guard where they saw bullet holes to the head as well as chest of the dead that were decaying after being put down.

"It looks like the national guard were here when things beginning to fall in the city, it looks like it was a tough fight and it was close quarters."

"Yeah, it looks like the fighting here was more like a rout and lots of people died as well as mistakes." Said Carter as he examined personal items that were left behind in the rush and the horror that people probably saw as those that were hotel rooms were being torn apart by the dead. Carter noticed there were security cameras at every hallway they walked through and if they were able to restore power to the hotel, those cameras could record the footage of the training. However, they would need to find the generators and if need be clear the generator room out if there were zombies that were there, they hadn't cleared the entire building just portions. They continued walking through the hotel which was in the heart of the historic district however it was a Marriot hotel, as they explored more the city and they realized that some of the buildings were damaged but many of them were miraculously untouched. The three of them finished looking through the Marriot hotel and exited the structure, all three of them didn't need to say anything but knew that they would need to clear out the rest of the building including the lower levels.

"What should we do about the two prisoners?"

"You and your sister as well as Randall take the two prisoners with you, drop them off at a town or a school that is far away from the farm. When you place a bag over their heads, use a mp3 player or an iPod to blast loud music into their hears so they can't hear what is being discussed. I can come with you and provide some backup, in case there is trouble." Said Marcus and they agreed to release the prisoners in a town or a school.

9

CHAPTER 7

At dawn, Marcus helped load the two prisoners into the back of a Savannah Police transport van and shackled them as they were wearing headphones with music blaring in their ears. Marcus was wearing a gray button-down shirt with short sleeves and was wearing brown cargo pants, in his right holster was his colt python magnum revolver and to his left pocket was his switchblade. Carter Dixon and Martha Dixon were equipped with their weapons as well as dressed wearing their leather jacket that had the patches of their motorcycle club. The two of them on the back of the leather jacket had a Cerberus dog and Latin words for defender on the bottom. Carter having left Atlanta behind him had kept his swat uniform in a place of safe keeping but no longer wore the uniform with pride, he had embraced what he was before and away from the city as a tracker as well as a hunter. Randall Welsch was standing next to Marcus with his t-shirt that revealed his muscular form, his facial hair was beginning to form and was growing a beard. Randall had his shotgun and in his right side was his holster for his pistol, Marcus got into the driver side as Randall followed into the passenger side. Carter and Martha Dixon got on their motorcycles as they followed behind the Police transport van. They exited the historic district and from there drove out of Savannah headed up north away from the city, in the cupholder of the drive side of the vehicle was Aiden's radio where they waited for his leader to contact him.

The small convoy headed on US highway 80 West; behind them the two prisoners were gagged as well as cuffed but also shackled to the chairs they were sitting on. Their ears were protesting in pain as the music blared loudly as they listened through headphones, they both were moaning as well as groaning. Marcus when he saw Aiden knew that he wouldn't want to mess with Carter or his siblings through the physical torture he sustained, his friend Courtney was slapped around by Martha who looked like she was in a bar fight. Marcus and Randall didn't say a word to each other, Marcus had nothing more to say after Randall called his wife a whore and was pushing him to make calls that knew that would cost the group everything. Randall looked out the passenger side window to see a sea of grass where he saw thirty to maybe forty zombies that were roaming together into the wooded area, he wondered where they were heading or if they had found an animal to eat. Randall and Marcus almost froze as they heard Aiden's radio crackle to life as someone spoke who was a man with a smoker's voice.

"Aiden and Courtney where are you to and what the fuck is taking you so damn long to get back after your supply run! You dumb bitch, if you got yourself killed by the dead then I hope you riot like the rest of these sorry worthless bags of rotting shit! We are getting ready to move out and head to Mexico if you are coming then hurry your lazy fucking ass over to the farm or I'll come over and drag you myself!" said the man who had a smoker's voice and sounded like he was rough.

Marcus kept his eye on the road as Randall heard the radio go back to static, they both knew that this could be a war between their groups. However, in Marcus's mind he made a silent vow that if anyone got between him and his family, he would kill and if he was threatened, he would kill.

The convoy followed the road signs to the town of Sylvania, as they passed by old car wrecks along the way or old army checkpoints. They stopped so that the prisoners while having a bag over their head as well as a blindfold, Marcus and Randall watched the prisoners as they relived themselves as well as being given water. Marcus turned his head to the right to see a roamer approach them, Marcus went into his left pocket and pulled out his switchblade as he pulled the blade out which was 3-inch blade. He walked over to the roamer and blocked the roamer's right arm from grabbing him as he used his left hand to stab the blade into the zombie's skull killing it. Marcus let the body fall as he walked away and placed the blade back after wiping the zombie's blood onto his pants.

"I think its better, from now on to use our knives. Guns attract the dead and knives are quiet." Said Marcus and saw that Carter as well as Martha nodded their heads. Marcus noticed Randall roll his eyes before nodding in agreement, Marcus knew that he had a sense of stubborn pride than most people. The prisoners were loaded back into the transport van and the convoy continued until they arrived at a town.

Sylvania,

Ga

Marcus held onto the hand-held radio that belonged to Aiden and turned clicked the side button so he could speak.

"If you can hear my voice then I have two of your people, Aiden and Courtney are alive and well. I'm not going to hurt them or kill them because we are all going to do things that we are going to regret in this world. I propose this, you and your group can leave for Mexico where you could find a place to live...to survive. But we don't have to fight and kill one another over pointless things, you can come meet us face to face in Sylvania and we could part ways." Said Marcus as he heard nothing but static until that same voice from before spoke again with that deep raspy smoker voice into the radio.

"You captured two of my people, I'll come meet you and I'll handle you myself dickface." Said the man on the radio who hadn't revealed his name. Marcus clicked the radio off and opened the back door of the van, he climbed into the back and pulled the hood off Aiden as well as the earphones.

"Does your leader have a raspy voice, like he used to smoke a lot."

"Yeah, he does, did you speak to him?"

"Yeah, and he is coming here."

"Then you should be afraid." Said Aiden before Marcus punching Aiden in the face before placing the hood over his head as well as the earphones back so he could hear the heavy metal band scream into his ears. He exited the back of the police van and waited for Aiden and Courtney's group to come for their people, Marcus knew in the back of his mind that there would be a fight between them.

"Alright listen up, we are about to have some company and let's get ready to defend ourselves." Said Marcus as he helped everyone set up traps, Carter lured some of the dead into a bar and locked the door before leaving. Randall helped Martha flip some outside tables for cover as Marcus backed the transport van over near Baptist Church.

They stopped as they heard the small group of the dead banging on the windows over in the bar as well as on the doors trying to get out. Once everything in order, they waited and the prisoners were away from the battle for now. Marcus placed his hand on his colt python magnum and waited knowing that he would have to kill again, he didn't want to and maybe he could still be diplomatic about the whole situation to find a more peaceful means. They were listening and headed into a building where they planned to meet this group of murders.

Marcus stood near the bar with Randall who sat in the chair drinking his whiskey, Carter sat drinking beer from a bottle and Martha was finishing her cigarette. They stopped when they heard two vehicles stop as six guys and one of them being a female exited what appeared to be a ford truck. The small group entered the bar each of them seeing the small group before them sitting around like the world hadn't ended, Marcus reacted to the people who entered as he slowly placed his hand against the butt of his colt python.

"Where are Aiden and Courtney?"

"They are safe for right now." Said Randall as he turned around on his chair to look at the people who had just arrived, the air was thick with tension and it everyone was bracing themselves for a shootout. Carter got up after finishing his drink and placed his crossbow on the table, his sister Martha finished the cigarette and kept her left-hand hovering over her pistol, the ones that were sent to search for Aiden and Courtney reacted the same way. The lead man who was heavyset African American pulled out a small revolver and was shot in the head by Marcus who didn't waste any time, the bar began to turn into a shootout like a wild west movie and Marcus's group flipped over tables as the ones who started the fight retreated to find better cover.

Marcus's group watched as the five members of the local group of raiders took cover behind the bar where the dead were stored inside in which had broken through the bar's door and some of the dead ran towards them where they focused their gunfire onto the dead. Marcus took cover behind the bar's counter as the sounds of gunshots was overwhelming and waited as the sounds of screaming continued. Randall peered from his cover and saw four of the dead were put down, he watched to see the woman within the group head to the direction of the Baptist church. Martha exited from her cover and followed the woman that was looking for her comrades, the rest exited the cover of the bar and took cover behind two parked cars as they used the dead to hide their advance. However, in the distance hearing gunfire a small herd numbering around three hundred zombies were heading towards the town of Sylvania. Randall fire rounds from his shotgun before reloading, Marcus fired his colt python magnum before reloading and Carter used his pistol. The sound of the guns that were being fired was almost deafening, there was empty shell cases all over the bar's wooden floors. The dead African American with a bullet to his head laid motionless as blood surrounded his lifeless corpse, Marcus knew that the man wouldn't turn because he was shot in the head. The dead that had broken through from being trapped were almost wiped out by the attackers, Marcus and Carter were back-to-back as they worked together. They worked as a united and they watched each other's back to defeat their enemies, Marcus holstered his weapon as he fought one of the raiders hand to hand. The man that Marcus fought was physically stronger than he was and had some training, however he took the blows like a man and countered them when he needed to. The man was heavyset and muscular as he grabbed Marcus by the throat and slammed him hard against the concrete where he started to strangle Marcus, Marcus instinctively trapped his assailant's arms to allow him a bit more breathing room. Marcus's assailant tried to pull his arms away from the trap block but he had other plans, Marcus using both his own strength as well as the skill broke his assailant's arms before he in one fluid motion got up and snapped his assailant's neck.

Martha followed the woman and saw that she found the transport van and had managed to get Aiden as well as Courtney out but was trying to free Aiden, she crouched behind some bushes and holstered her weapon as she unsheathed her hunting knife. Martha Dixon moved as quiet as she could and grabbed the woman from behind as she stabbed her in the kidney before slicing her slicing her Achilles heel. The woman screamed in pain before she could finish freeing Courtney, however Martha was like a panther. However, the woman still fought back against Martha but her strength was fading, the woman slashed with her own knife into Martha's right leg and had a slash across her left forearm. Martha screamed in pain as if she was banshee, but continued to fight on using her knife as an extension of herself. The fight continued before Martha finished the woman who she didn't care meeting or knowing her name before slashing her throat.

The sole survivor of the battle against Marcus's group tried to crawl away who was shot three times, one in the right shoulder and the other in the left shoulder as well as the third wound he sustained was a shotgun shot to his right kneecap. The man moaned and cried in pain as he dragged himself forward as there was a blood trail leading from, he started to where he was now, the wounded man had tattoos that from Marcus and Randall knew was former gang affiliations. Marcus

Wayne walked over with his colt python magnum in his hands and placed his cowboy boot onto the weapon he was trying to reach which was a pistol a 9mm.

"I'll tell you what, I am willing to offer your group mercy after your pal raised a weapon against me. Your friend started something that I didn't want to start and now I am going to finish it, you could have survived till the end and built a life with your people in Mexico away from all this. But you started something, you threatened me and my people." Said Marcus as he pointed the barrel of his colt python magnum to the head of the tattooed man who was stopped from reaching a fallen pistol. The tattooed man coughed up blood, his eyes showed nothing but fear and the realization that his time was over. Marcus Wayne looked at the body of the man whose neck was snapped began to get up as he reanimated.

"No don't put him down, leave him for this guy." Said Marcus as he holstered his weapon and picked up the fallen pistol, Marcus and the three men left the skirmish they had fought as they headed to find Martha. As they walked away, the man who was shot three times screamed in horror as the reanimated raider who had his neck snapped was bitten on his arm before his screams were silenced when the zombie bit into his neck.

Marcus Wayne, Randall Welsch and Carter Dixon arrived to find Martha Dixon with blood covering her shirt and her leather jacket as well as the corpse of the woman whose throat was slashed, the prisoners were cut lose but still had their handcuffs on as well as their blindfolds leaving them to roam without vision.

"Martha are you okay?" asked Carter who knelt beside his sister who was trembling after the fight and was knelt by the body of the woman she had killed who was starting to reanimate. Martha nodded her head as she was ushered with Carter to their bikes because in the silent town, they could hear the dead approaching, which meant they would have no way out if they were encircled. Randall closed the back of the van and got into the passenger seat as Marcus drove away from the town, as the Dixons followed behind them on their motorcycles. As they drove away from the town, the small herd of the dead numbering three hundred roamed the city. Marcus used his left hand to wipe away the blood that was smeared on his face and looked into the rearview mirror to see his face was covered in the blood of those that he killed or the dead he killed.

Maggie Wayne continued to practice reloading her 9mm pistol as she was just shooting her targets, once she reloaded her weapon, she fired at another target which was a coffee cup then tracked her weapon to a wine bottle. The two targets a wine bottle and the coffee cup shattered as the bullets hit them, Maggie Wayne was slowly becoming a good shot and was even getting quicker at reloading her gun. She was getting better through her husband's teachings as well as Carter's teachings of breaching doors as well as sweeping rooms, she was being taught hand to hand combat from Martha Dixon as well as Carter. Maggie Wayne through her husband's wisdom as well as teachings was making a better survivor, as well as the teachings from Carter and Martha Dixon as well as their brother Atticus who taught her how to kill the dead in close quarters combat. She had clipped to her waist was the radio that her husband gave her in order to keep in contact with the group as well as report anything that was out of the ordinary. She knew her husband had left early in the morning with the two prisoners from another group that were going to be cut loose, she finished target practice and holstered her weapon as she walked away from the target practice which was set up outside of a nearby catholic church. In the distance she could smell fires burning as some of the group were preparing the food that was fished from the sea as well as cooking the contents from cans. The survivors were hard at work as they prepared for the journey up north to Missouri, some of the survivors scavenged for snow chains as well as further supplies such as food and water. The other survivors were on watch as they used hunting rifles as snipers and peered through windows as well as binoculars to see if anything was approaching. Maggie Wayne noticed a survivor who was quiet at most times but some were able to gather information that he used to be a former corrections officer watched the roads leading into the historic district with his sniper rifle, he kept his eyes focused on the environment before him. She continued to walk and arrived at the local hotel where her husband as well as her son slept, she was the temporary leader of the group until her husband returned. Marcus had taught his wife many things in terms of leadership as well as how to keep an open mind while also being able to speak clearly when issues needed to be discussed. The survivors were also preparing for war in the event those raiders attacked them, they had amassed guns and ammunition from the various police stations as well as old national guard checkpoints. The city of Savannah was hit not so hard but the horrors were present, nobody knew the exact toll of the deaths that was wrought when the dead walked. She walked through the lobby and heard her hiking boots clumped against the marble stone floor, as she walked up the stairs to the room where her husband slept and sat down on the bed. She was tired and she knew just a taste of what her husband has gone through with the demands of leadership, she was worried for him at times but she knew he was trying his best. She knew her husband was strong and brave as well as a leader who was able to be there for his group.

Marcus Wayne returned to the historic district of Savannah and walked into the hotel as he returned to the war table as he studied the map once again. He looked at the map as afternoon turned to evening, he turned on the lanterns as he studied the map and felt once again like he was in the military.

"So, what's the next step in this war?" asked Carter as he stepped out of the shadows and walked over to the war table, Marcus looked at Carter who was dressed in the same clothes as he wore in the morning. Carter's face no longer had the blood on it or Marcus's face, the two were joined by Martha Dixon as well as Randall Welsch as all three studied the map.

"How long will we be ready in case they attack us?"

"Two weeks at most, but we will be ready. They started the fight and we are going to finish it, an eye for an eye."

"Martha, why don't you take some snipers to cover the main road leading into Savannah while your brother Atticus takes a group to cover the other roads leading to Savannah while we prepare for both evacuation and defensive strategies. "said Randall Welsch as Martha her nodded after giving a brief look at Marcus who nodded his head in agreement, the plan was get ready for both a defensive and offensive strategy. Marcus added his own emphasis on the strategy that Carter, Randall and himself would lead the offensive assault on the farm to finish the fight. It was time to finish the fight that was started by the raiders. Marcus exited the meeting and walked out of the office into a small hotel courtyard as he began to ponder the man he was becoming, that his moral code needed to be expanded upon as well as improved upon.

"What have I become? "asked Marcus to himself as the events of today spiraled into his mind, he had killed in self defense and he knew it wasn't something that people should never celebrate. It was now the way of the world to Survive or Die, it was the world had become and the insanity that followed with it.

10

CHAPTER 8

In the early hours and into the early afternoon, Marcus oversaw the training of his wife as well as other members of his group in hand-to-hand combat as well as polishing how to clear out rooms. They had preformed well and they were becoming experienced in record breaking time, Marcus followed as he watched his wife closely who had taken the lead with her small squad of being three adults each of them armed with automatic rifles and checked their corners as they approached the fire exit of the Marriot Hotel. Marcus and everyone else heard the dead inside the building as they moaned and groaned as well as snarled, this was the first of their final tests before they were able to defend themselves.

Maggie Wayne was dressed in a jacket as well as a short-sleeved shirt, she wore on her feet hiking boots and was ready for combat. She had in a sheathe a knife and in her left holster was her pistol, in her hands was a MP5 submachine gun with a suppressor screwed tightly on the barrel. Maggie Wayne gently opened the door as she turned on the flashlight on her MP5 and entered the building through the fire exit, she swept left and right as she scanned the area around her. She moved with careful precision and fired two shots at a roamer killing it when the second shot penetrated through the skull, she paused every so often to allow those that followed her time to conduct the same ritual she did. It was almost becoming second nature, an instinct in her ability to clear rooms one by one. She cleared the kitchen as she swept her weapon from left to right, and used her training as a guide.

Carter Dixon had managed to get some of the monitors as well as cameras working, as he examined the monitors and watched the security cameras. He was impressed by Maggie Wayne at how far she had come since the beginning and was becoming a professional. He knew that Maggie Wayne was getting stronger and she would only continue to get stronger, he was proud of her and knew that she would be needed in other times of struggle.

Randall Welsch was dressed in a t-shirt that clearly showed his muscular body, he oversaw the construction of sandbags as well as reconstructing the bridge Robert Smalls Parkway. He could hear the waves crashing against the rocks, the sound of seagulls as they flew in the air. However, the flow of repairs and construction stopped as Randall found some binoculars as he heard dead approach, he turned his head to the right and the left to see that the survivors stopped working as they froze.

"What the fuck?" said Randall as he looked up from the binoculars to see the herd that was in Sylvania Ga arrive and numbering around four hundred to maybe six hundred zombies, Randall yelled orders to those that were helping with repairs on the parkway bridge and grabbing his walkie talkie that a herd has arrived at the city of Savannah.

"We need everyone up to the front, we have sighted a massive herd numbering between four hundred to six hundred zombies! I repeat this isn't a drill and we need everyone now!" shouted Randall into the walkie talkie as he grabbed his shotgun that was resting on the hood of a car before charging forward as the herd moved slowly through the city. Every survivor knew that if the dead were approaching and the sounds of guns firing would draw more the dead to them, which in conclusion would mean that there would be no way out. Randall was the first that fired his weapon into the dead aiming for the head as best as he could, one of the zombies grabbed him causing Randall to stumble back before using the butt of his shotgun to hit the zombie in the head. He pointed the barrel of his shotgun and fired the gun that blew out the chest of the zombie who was dressed in an old post office worker, the post office worker zombie stumbled backwards with his chest blown out before Randall fired once again into the zombie's hip which was blown out. He continued to open fire and stepped back as he reloaded his weapon before firing once again.

Marcus Wayne sprinted towards the radio call as well as the sounds of gunfire, he unholstered his colt python magnum as he sprinted towards the horror that had arrived at the city of Savannah. He sprinted from where he was at the Marriot hotel past shops and residential buildings as well as burnt cars, his heart was racing as he sprinted like a race horse. He heard gunfire that were getting closer as well as the growls of the dead, he didn't stop running until he climbed an alley fence of a house before joining the firing line. Marcus fired his colt python magnum into what used to be a woman and she was wearing a teacher's outfit that had dried blood around her cloth's neck opening. He fired the bullet that hit the former teacher in the shoulder before firing a second shot into her head killing the reanimated teacher once again with a secondary death. Marcus watched as Randall fired his shotgun before discarding the weapon as he drew out his pistol before continuing to open fire, they were soon joined by Maggie Wayne and Carter Dixon as well as Martha Dixon and Atticus Dixon who joined their fire onto the herd. They stepped back as they reloaded their weapons before firing once again, they were soon joined by the rest of the survivors as they opened fire with their weapons or used melee weapons which were quieter. The dead were dropping as they were shot or stabbed in the head, upon Marcus's orders they holstered their guns or they slung their guns over their shoulders before grabbing their melee weapons. Marcus grabbed a zombie who by the clothes he was wearing was once a doctor and noticed his badge that was clipped to his lab coat, he threw punches at the zombie who was snarling as well as groaning but he wondered if the dead could feel pain. As he threw punches at the zombie, he in one fluid motion broke the zombie's right arm before delivering a powerful side kick to the zombie's right leg which brought the zombie down. Marcus as the zombie was on its left knee was kicked hard onto the street by Marcus delivering a powerful kick with his left leg to the zombie's chest, the zombie tried to get back up but was brought down again with a powerful kick to its face. Marcus knelt pinning the zombie's left arm before using his switchblade to stab the zombie's skull killing it once again. He got up not knowing that he was covered in the blood of the zombies he had killed, he used his blade with precision and slowly building up his skill.

Carter Dixon grabbed one of the zombies and flipped it over his shoulder before kicking its skull killing the zombie once again, as he used his knives as well as strength to overtake the threats that were before him. Carter Dixon used both his strength as well as his endurance to overtake the threats, as well as keeping his field of vision aware of the surroundings. The streets were almost drowned in the blood of the dead, as well as the streets were clogged with the bodies of the dead that were put down. Carter turned his head momentarily to see his brother Atticus pick up a zombie as he slammed it hard against the hood of a car before stabbing its head, he saw his sister Martha shoot her gun at point blank into a zombie which was a child. The streets of Savannah were drowned in blood, sweat and tears, some of the survivors who were new to shooting guns were taken down by the dead as they were bitten and torn open.

The battle against the dead ended what seemed like two minutes but was in fact two hours, Marcus walked over to a zombie who was grazed by a gunshot before being put down permanently. He was exhausted and breathing hard after he exerted himself, he looked around to see his wife was drenched in the blood of the dead as well as everyone else. He also looked around to see that Carter was ending the reanimation process of those that were in his community that were killed. Marcus walked over to a zombie that was crawling, before Marcus plunged his blade into its head. He walked through the puddles of blood and bits of bone fragments as well as stepping on organs that were blown out by gunfire, Marcus stepped on an intestine and stepped on other bits of organs. The corpses were decided to be left there so that the crows could feed on the bodies, those that were members of the group after being put down were buried. Marcus sat on the third step of a store that was once a bookstore as he reloaded his Colt Python Magnum as his wife walked over to join him on the third step. Marcus moved over to allow room for his wife who hugged him before kissing him on the lips, the two smiled as Maggie Wayne reloaded her MP5.

"I think its time for us to end that group, we killed a lot of them when we were doing the prisoner transfer and we know where they are located." Said Randall as he walked over to Marcus and his wife, Marcus looked up to Randall with a glare but had to squint from the sun beaming onto his face.

"I'll decide when we do that Randall, for right now the threat is still around but they are becoming less of a threat. We have winter coming here soon and we have a trip to plan with the remaining members of our group to Saint Louis, I know that there is a place where we could settle down and rebuild our lives from what we had in the past. A place where we could grow crops, have clean water and manufacture our own supplies. I have a feeling of a place of a golden land so to speak where we could survive the rest of our lives." Said Marcus as he got up and in the deepest corners of his mind, he knew that there was a place where they could be able to live in peace as well as have plenty to eat. Randall walked away to gather up some people to finish off the raiders, Marcus knew that Randall was going to get himself into trouble and they never knew the defenses of the farm or if they were trying to locate where they were.

Randall gathered Atticus Dixon and ten other survivors as they drove out of Savannah in a convoy to where the raiders had set up camp.

During the evening, Marcus Wayne, Carter Dixon and Martha Dixon would go to Kachina Farms as well to end the threat.

11

Chapter 9

Outside of Kachina Farms

It was early afternoon when Marcus and his small force joined Randall's force for the all-out assault against the raider's base of operations, since they defended Savannah against a herd and created noise while doing so, they spotted a herd growing to become a horde which would be tens of thousands of zombies clustered together. They could hear from where they were the sounds of dead moaning and growling as the wind carried their sounds to the ears of Marcus's survivors. Marcus's survivors prepared for either open warfare or for ambush style raids onto their base of operations, Marcus wished he had a special forces group on hand who could tell him the defenses that were emplace as well as how many were on perimeter patrol. They were a good distance away and had established their own field base before preparing to attack or to defend if they were spotted, they had perfect cover with trees that protected them from line of sight as well as tall grass. Marcus Wayne sat on the driver side of a ford truck as he checked his Colt Python Magnum revolver and went into his shirt pocket, he found a family picture of his family at the opening of a steakhouse and had their picture taken. He smiled remembering that day when everything was normal and there wasn't this constant feeling of fear or despair in people's eyes, he smiled seeing his lovely wife with her pristine white skin and her beautiful smile with red lipstick on her lips. He smiled as she saw his wife's beautiful eyes that were brown in color. He loved his wife and he looked at the little man, his son who was still scared and he hoped that through his wisdom as well as his guidance that when something happened to him that his son would takeover leadership. However, Marcus knew that Connor still needed to be a boy and needed to get his general education either from reading books or being taught by a teacher, Marcus's first lesson to his son about being a leader was to always have knowledge and to use it as guidance.

Marcus folded the picture in half and placed it back into his shirt pocket before exiting the driver's side of the truck. He walked over to Carter Dixon who was doing his ritual as he had laid out in front of him was his M4A1 automatic rifle as he stripped the weapon, as he started to clean it before placing it back together. Carter was busy working but heard Marcus's cowboy boots crunch on the leaves as well as twigs that had fallen, it was starting to get colder and winter was approaching.

"Carter, I have a plan and I feel like when it gets dark. We could and a few others scout out the threat before we eliminate it. "

"Yeah, sounds like a good plan, but Marcus I am going to say something that may get you upset and I apologize. But when we were in that bar, you killed someone and we all did but I thought you wanted the living to fight the dead for us to unite against a common threat. Are you sure okay with what we are about to do? "asked Carter and looked up to Marcus who gathered his thoughts before speaking,

Carter thought Marcus was going to be angry with him or banish him from the group however that wasn't the case.

"I know Carter, but the man who I killed was going to kill me or you or anybody who is going to be fighting with us. I still believe in us the living fighting against the dead, however more to the point those people are animals and there aren't the police anymore so we have to rebuild the world in the way we imagine it. Fuck these animals and anyone who is like them, we don't celebrate their deaths or take pleasure from it and we certainly don't kill those who haven't crossed us first or attack someone without being struck first. Violence and war are the last measure when all other options have been removed from the field of play, they attacked us Carter first and we defended ourselves so they will be defeated." Said Marcus who was calmly justifying the action as well as imparting some wisdom onto Carter, Marcus was already planning that if something were to happen to him his son Connor would lead and Carter would be the second in command of the group. Carter nodded his head and got up from the fallen tree branch he was sitting on before slinging his rifle over his shoulder, Marcus returned the nod and gave a smile to his friend.

When evening approached and night began to fall across the sky. Marcus Wayne, Carter Dixon, Atticus Dixon, Martha Dixon and Randall Welsch crouched as they moved through the wooded area before arriving outside of the farm to hear voices from the raiders who were camped. Marcus waved a series of hand signals to pass orders around to those who were clustered around him, Randall Welsch took the left as well as Atticus and Martha Dixon. Marcus and Carter moved right to scout out the perimeter as well as cause some damage. They moved like predators as they stalked around the perimeter of the camp before making entry, Marcus Wayne and Carter Dixon climbed a white fence before taking cover behind a tractor. Both Marcus and Carter heard a man speak to someone on the radio as he was patrolling the area, they both froze as they blended with the environment around them as the natural darkness surrounded them. Marcus when the man began to walk away from the tractor did, he come up behind him and covered his mouth before slitting his throat. Carter rounded the corner of the cover and followed Marcus as he watched walking past the body twitch as the last of the man's life ebbed away. Marcus and Carter spotted and took cover behind a barn as they heard four people talking around a barrel that they were using for warmth, the two of them noticed that further they went into the farm the more defenses that had hastily erected. Marcus spotted sandbags, a building that was the secondary barn for what appeared to be ammo as well as fuel storage and the third barn was being used for food as well as water storage.

Randall Welsch moved like a ninja in the dark and came up behind a man who was probably in his mid to late thirties before snapping his neck, Randall dragged the body behind a broken-down truck from the mid-1960s before continuing with Atticus and marking areas of interest into his memory for further briefings. Randall Welsch and Atticus Dixon moved with stealth as they took out threats by using silent takedowns, once they were with gathering their evidence did, they fall back to wait for Marcus and Carter who arrived behind them ten minutes later. When they returned to camp, they heard the raiders come alive with gunfire as well as screams as those that were killed by the scouting party had turned. They all that they would be busy with the dead and would slowly begin to run dry on ammo, the key in every war was to cut off the supply lines as well as cause as much damage to the enemy to break them either causing terror or by physical damage.

Within the camp, they could hear in the distance the sound of gunfire and people shouting that more are coming. From what they were hearing gunfire had attracted a small herd of roamers that were coming towards the farm. Marcus Wayne stood on the roof of a truck under a full moon sky, he investigated binoculars to see the raiders desperately trying to defend their territory from a small herd that was causing damage into the group. Marcus knew that his wife was worried about him that he was beginning to change like everyone else was changing to the new world, the key of humanity was that we adapted or we died falling into the dustbin of history as an extinct species. The siege with the raiders against the dead continued well into the morning as Marcus's survivors gathered their strength instead of sleeping preparing for the outcome.

The morning after, Marcus Wayne and Randall Welsch did not sleep with their experience of having overnight watches or doing undercover operations. Marcus Wayne and Randall Welsch gathered their strength as they moved the same way they did the night before, the gunfire stopped as well as the screams in the early morning. Marcus unholstered his Colt Python Magnum and fired a single shot into the early morning sky alerting what remained of the raiders that some-body had arrived. They waited as they took cover behind a chicken coop as well as the horse's stable, they saw the lights were on over in the main house which sat in the middle of the array of buildings and heard the voices of ten men as well as one woman who were the raiders.

"Listen you must be the assholes who captured Aiden and Court-ney when we found them, they were dead, along with the party we sent to recover them and then last night we had intruders who caused us a bit of a stir with the dead knocking on our door. It seems like this little game of ours is coming to an end, but it doesn't have to end and maybe we could join our groups together."

"We didn't kill Aiden and Courtney, but we killed the party that you sent to find them and you were the ones who started this battle when I found Aiden and Courtney, they tried to kill me. I acted in pure self defense and I am going to offer you the same chance I offered your party that you sent to find them. You can leave now and go to Mexico; you never return to this place or any place and I promise that we will never hunt you down! I promise that your group and mine will live in peace, maybe you get lucky and find a place where you could survive all this. This doesn't have to be your end, it's us against the dead and we must do our parts in this insane world. I know that you have killed people and that you have raided, But I am offering this one chance to you against my own thoughts for you to change and leave for Mexico! My people have spilled enough blood from you and I won't hesitate to act in self defense again." Said Marcus Wayne from behind cover as he looked around the farm seeing the blood-soaked earth, the bodies lying on the bare dirt and the buzzing of flies as they began to eat the corpses on the ground. The farm was built a long time ago and the fields were empty of corps. They waited for an answer in the heat of the Georgia sun, after awhile Marcus spotted the door opening with hands raised. Carter Dixon and his siblings covered Marcus as he stepped out of cover approaching the man who had no weapon. Marcus stopped and placed his hand on the butt of his Colt python as the man who had a short-sleeved shirt approached before throwing down his holstered pistol as well as sheathed knife to the ground.

"We agree to your terms, you won and you defeated us. We will leave as soon as possible; our blood has already been spilled and we no longer have the desire to fight." Said the man who spoke with conviction as well as honesty.

"What is your name? "asked Marcus Wayne to the man who was standing before him as if he was conquering king to a man who was bested in combat.

"My name is Luke and Matthew is inside, please I'm sorry." Said Luke as he began to tear up realizing all the wrong, he had done, the raping and the murdering of communities. Marcus ordered that the supplies would be divided evenly and the two communities would no longer have any bad blood between them. Marcus helped up Luke who was a younger man in his twenties and watched as his followers were disarmed before Marcus's followers gathered half of the supplies. Marcus looked at Carter and Martha who nodded their heads that the threat had been dealt with that there was nothing else to fear.

However, both Randall and Atticus were the only ones who silently voicing their nays to what had transpired, they knew that they should be dealt with and brought to extinction like the animals they were instead of offering them mercy. In Randall's eyes this lack of common sense baffled him and knew that he would be the one to lead by dispensing the threats that would arise, he was fit for the coming days when his leadership was assured to begin. The two of them walked back to camp ashamed and feeling like they lost a battle and an entire war, they arrived at camp and drove away in the direction of Savannah.

Marcus Wayne, Carter Dixon and Martha Dixon watched as the raiders who were granted mercy were getting into their vehicles to depart for their voyage to Mexico. The three of them watched as the trucks left the farm and headed onto the main road.

"So, I guess we won the war against those people, I know what you did Marcus was showing your mercy and I was worried for you at that bar. I never saw you act in the way you did last time, but it was good you decided to spare them and from what I have seen they took damage from us as well as the dead. They will be licking their wounds for a longtime, they will no longer have the strength to defend themselves against a living threat or the dead." Said Martha Dixon who spoke with conviction as well as clarity in her choice of words as if she was a politician speaking from experience.

"I'm sorry Martha, I didn't mean for you see that and I hope that they will not ruin the second chance I have given them, that they themselves would turn away from what they had done. This group we are the ones who live and we tell ourselves that we survive or we die, we tell ourselves to never lose our humanity and we aren't the Walking Dead because we choose to survive, because we are the ones who live." Said Marcus Wayne as he looked at Carter and Martha Dixon the ones who placed their trust in him as a leader.

Once they had watched the defeated group of raiders leave, did Marcus and his closet lieutenants left for their camp to drive away back towards Savannah.

Randall Welsch, Atticus Dixon and those that joined him waited as the defeated raiders drove their vehicles along the road. They had left spikes on the road and waited to finish them off, they would make it look as though it was the dead who got them rather than the living. Randall counted down silently to himself, they had hidden their vehicles to make it as though it was a car wreck that had been there for a longtime. When Randall counted down to twelve did Atticus and another survivor pull the spikes as soon as the vehicles drove over them causing the front as well as the back wheels to spin out of control. The cars crashed and caused two of them to flip over off the road or another one to crash into a tree, within seconds of causing nothing but destruction did Randall Welsch begin to finish off the raiders who had survived. Randall Welsch spotted the young man Luke crawl away who was covered in scraps as well as cuts, he walked over as he followed the blood trail avoiding the slaughter that was being done. Luke turned over when Randall gave him a hard kick to the right side of his ribs causing him to flip onto his back, Randall didn't feel pity nor mercy when he gave Luke the hardest kick that felt as if the earth itself had shaken violently.

"Please your leader had given me mercy, I don't want to die please have mercy." Said Luke as tears began to form and fall like a waterfall, Randall Welsch gave nothing a bloodthirsty smile before he sat on his stomach and placed the shotgun onto his neck to strangle Luke. The last words of Luke were muttered as his life was beginning to slip as he was being strangled, Luke tried to claw at Randall's face but to no avail and his death would only be furthered by more pain. Randall used his strength as he looked up to see the dead had been attracted to the car crash as well as the screams of the dying, he smiled at Luke who was struggling to breathe as well as fight back against a man who was more physically fit than he was. He was surprised to be sure that Luke was holding on for this long as the dead began to approach, Luke's eyes turned to the left as a roamer approached them with a gaze of terror. Randall in one fluid motion let go as he grabbed the shirt of the roamer and pulled it onto Luke who screamed in agony as it torn into his neck. Randall Welsch and those that followed him began to walk away from the slaughter, there was blood that was beginning to flow like a river and oil mixing with the blood. They gathered the spikes from the road and got into their vehicles to leave the sight of the ambush, a sense of calm passed over Randall as a sense of true peace.

12

CHAPTER 10

It was early morning or who could say when a rainstorm arrived onto Georgia, rain pounded against the roofs of many buildings and the rain when breathed in so clean as if mother nature was recovering from decades of pollution. It had been two days since Marcus Wayne, Carter Dixon and Martha Dixon discovered the car crash of the raiders along their return trip to Savannah, He had never seen that scale of devastation before and the smell was vile, the smell of oil and the coppery smell of blood mixing together. They all felt like apart of them had been torn out, as if they were losing their humanity after viewing the aftermath of a crash that costed the lives of a group that were once bad but were being redeemed to be better than they were. Marcus repeated what he told Martha and Carter that they were the ones who live, it was becoming a source of strength to repeat those words as if he was keeping them sane as the world around them had embraced insanity.

Marcus was asleep with his wife and was tossing around, as the nightmares of when he was a soldier were returning once again. He broke free from the nightmare when he woke up as a bolt of lightning arced across the sky and the rain hit the glass window, he turned his head to see his wife was sleeping peacefully and he smiled at her innocence. He looked to the window as the rain pattered against the glass and the room brightened when a bolt of lightning arced the sky, he slowly got up from the bed careful not to wake his wife and walked to the hotel room's adjoining door to where Connor his son slept who was asleep peacefully. He took a deep breath and felt a sense of calm wash over him, everyone within his group were losing how many months and days it had been since the fall. He being true to himself believed he was losing track and felt as if the days were blending. He walked over to the bathroom and turned on the light, he was dirty and he hadn't showered for a longtime. He removed his t-shirt and his boxer shorts before turning on the shower as water flowed, it felt good to have running water and power. He felt the warm water against his white skin and his brown hair, he closed his eyes as the warmth of the water ran down his shoulders.

Maggie Wayne woke up to hear the water running and opened the door as she removed her clothes, she gently opened the glass door and joined her husband in the shower. She closed her eyes to feel the warmth of the water and how great it felt, in front of her was her husband whom she kissed his back and then his lips as the two of them looked into each other's eyes. The two let out an exhale of pleasure as their bodies wrapped together and shared in passionate sex in the shower, it had been so long since they had sex and it released memories, they wanted to forget by replacing them with better memories. Maggie's right hand was placed against the glass sliding door of the shower as Marcus's penis slide into her and her legs wrapped around her husband's waist, she moaned in pleasure as he made love to her. The early morning ended with Marcus and Maggie Wayne leaving the shower as the two got dressed in their clothes, she felt happy after she made love with her husband.

Marcus Wayne after seeing his wife out of the door who was getting her first day on guard duty, he walked over to wake up their son who needed to go to school to become an intelligent person. Once he got his son up from bed and helped him get dress did, he walks with his son to a building that was converted into a school. It was a normal day and preparations were almost finish to leave for Saint Louis Missouri, he had scouts mark areas where the dead had congregated as red zones. The rain continued as Marcus Wayne walked the cobblestone streets and nodded his head to those that remained within his group, they were armed with rifles and automatic weapons and had used barrels to create fires to keep warm. It was getting colder and winter was getting closer, nobody knew how the winter weather would affect the dead or if it affects them like a normal human.

He walked over and stopped when he saw Carter and Martha Dixon fixing their motorcycles inside an old garage, they were wearing their leather jackets of their respected motorcycle club. He stopped and grabbed a stool in which he sat on it and heard the tools clanking against the motorcycle.

"So, is everything ready for our departure to Saint Louis?"

"Yeah, everything is already to go and we will hopefully leave tomorrow. The route is marked and our plan is going from Savannah to Charleston South Carolina before looping around Atlanta then head into Memphis Tennessee and heading from Memphis to Saint Louis. We've gathered enough supplies with winter coats and food as well as water to last us, if we must stop it would be for fuel or other supplies or using the restroom. It should be an easy drive other than the dead if we encounter or the living we might encounter. It looks like the world is about to get a whole bigger and like you said Marcus it's about pulling together to rebuild the world. "said Carter as he finished making some repairs as well as adjustments to his motorcycle that had snow chains as all the other vehicles had them. Marcus saw that Martha Dixon was beginning to form a bit of sweat as she was working on making repairs as well as adjustments to her bike, it made him smile to see two siblings working together and made him remember about his siblings.

"You know, I have a brother and a sister. I still love them and I often think about them, the last family dinner we had was a phone call that my cousin and his brother had been deployed to Saudi Arabia to help train their soldiers in basic tactics like we did with our group. Anyway, that was the last time we spoke to my cousins and before that my brother and sister were deployed to Afghanistan. The one thing that I remember telling me is that when things get tough, it's always better to be on your toes and let your mind be your guide in those situations. "said Marcus Wayne before leaving the garage, outside their was the sound of belongings being transported into vehicles.

It was the calm before the road trip and the group knew they would miss the fresh sea air and the sound of the waves lapping against the rocks. However, it was time for the group to move out, to find a better prospect where they could prosper as well as survive. Marcus walked over to Randall who was placing his backpack and his gym bag onto the back of his truck, he stopped so Marcus could see him standing before him.

"Listen man, if you've come here to give one of your speeches you could fuck off. But if you're here to talk then I'll listen to you."

"Listen Randall, I know these past months and days have been difficult for us. But I want to know that for whatever had come between us as friends and as brothers that I would never forget that you were there at the hospital when I was woken up from my coma. I would not forget that you got my family and myself out of King James County Georgia, that it was you who taught me how to survive in this world. I just want you to know that we need not fight each other, that we can survive this by pulling together and not apart.

"I think that would be a good idea, I accept your apology Marcus but I feel like I was robbed of being leader of this group."

"I know and I am sorry Randall, maybe I could see if we could be joint leaders." Said Marcus trying to ease his friend's worry. After Marcus finished talking to Randall, walked back to the hotel to help his family with their belongings before loading them into the car.

All throughout the morning and into the evening did the survivors labor onwards with moving their belongings into their vehicles, during the early afternoon Randall and Marcus, Carter Dixon, Atticus Dixon, Martha Dixon, Maggie Wayne, Connor Wayne, Frederick and Rose drove to a facility that was a temporary CDC research building where he learned even more what Marcus talked about in those early days seeing for himself that everyone was infected and all that needn't happen is for people to die. In that facility they heard the same video in which Marcus listened already in the main headquarters of the CDC except there was more that had already been sent to other government facilities. The facility was running on emergency power and it was beginning to run low, they had minutes before the facility went dark.

"If you are listening to this, to any surviving members of the government or if you are a survivor in general. There will be a time when the days, years and months have gone dark in which you would not want to live anymore. The world's population has turned from living people to the dead, that is why I am saying this is our extinction event and be with your family when you decide to kill yourself because there will come a day when there will be no escape for the living. I hope to some of you who are brave and have decided to fight, I wish you the best of luck but I give you this warning there will be no escape for the living. I will say this like I said previously we are all infected." Said the CDC doctor before the video clicked off into static, everyone looked at one another with glances of both fear as well as sadness. As they were leaving the facility which was an old warehouse that was converted into a CDC field headquarters, slowly but surely the emergency power began to slow down as the lights began to fade into the darkness. The survivors finally understood the cost of what was happening, Frederick and Rose were the first to hear that everyone was infected that they had no clue that Marcus Wayne had heard it before them. But now the debate was settled and full realization that everyone was infected had settled, that all you had to do was die and then you turn to become a monster who no longer looked at their family with love but as food to sate their hunger. As the hours passed by, they returned to the historic district of Savannah and there was awkward silence as the survivors ate together in the hotel's restaurant, the rain had somewhat stopped but was still a constant however they knew the hour was fast approaching for the journey to Missouri.

13

Chapter 11

At the crack of dawn, Marcus's survivors returned to their vehicles for the journey towards Saint Louis where they hoped they could rebuild their lives as well as a place where they could enjoy a sense of safety. As the sun broke through the clouds of yesterday's rainstorm, the roar of the engines of the vehicles echoed along the brick and stone walls of the historic buildings of Savannah.

"Next Stop Saint Louis Missouri!" shouted Marcus Wayne as he opened his car door before following the Dixon siblings on their motorcycles out of the historic district of Savannah, those who didn't survive the brief war against the raiders or the brief battle against the dead who entered Savannah their vehicles were left behind as well as their belongings. However, those that were apart of Marcus's group and who had died along the way would forever be inscribed in the group's collective memory. As the group began their long journey towards Saint Louis, further away dark clouds were approaching as snow began to fall.

As the group headed away from Savannah, they drove past areas they hadn't seen such as military installations as well as checkpoints that were established. They drove past long abandoned military vehicles that were parked as well as supplies that were left behind, it seemed in their eyes that damage of this pandemic as well as the results of civil disorder caused wounds into the very soul of America that would take decades to heal. Marcus as he drove kept his eyes on the road as well as scanning the environment in which he was driving, he was keeping an eye out for threats as well as any obstructions that were placed along the road. They had just crossed the parkway bridge and were on course to head towards South Carolina, they had chosen the long way instead of going through Atlanta.

It was late morning when Marcus's band of survivors stopped in the tracks just outside of Charleston South Carolina. The storm had blotted out the sun as snow began to fall, it was getting colder and so the survivors put on winter clothes to help keep themselves warm. They had stopped because the first and second RV broke down, they were older RVs from the 90s and were no longer up to par like the modern-day RVs. Marcus Wayne was wearing his winter coat that had his station's name on it, he walked around keeping his eyes focused but it was difficult as the snow continued to fall it created poor visibility. As the survivors walked around outside there was a deep howl of the wind as the snowstorm raged, it was as if God was preventing them from leaving Georgia or making them return to the state. It was rare for South Carolina to have a massive snowstorm that seemed to have the next ice age behind it, however it was clearly an exaggeration of the storm and how it was bringing within the full force of winter.

After what felt like hours but was really thirty minutes, the RVs were repaired before continuing their journey and as visibility was getting worse, they had to turn on their high beam lights. As the survivors drove, they had to dodge old car wrecks or the occasional roamer who was wandering the streets, they were clearly in a small town or the suburbs of Charleston South Carolina. They continued until they reached the interior of Charleston which was war torn, the buildings that they could see were bombed out and their structural damage. The group of survivors continued through the city of Charleston, it was a ghost town and the snow provided an eerie feeling like it was an ancient city buried under the desert sands of Egypt. It was hours later when they exited the city of Charleston leaving behind the ghost town that also belonged to the dead. They were heading deeper into the state of South Carolina where they would hopefully find a place to stop for the night before continuing their journey to Saint Louis.

The snowstorm started to let up and the snowfall decreased with every hour and every minute, the clouds began to break as the sun fought to clear the skies and visibility was slowly returning but it was taking time. They continued slowly as they dodged the wrecks along the road as well as the damaged sections of the roads or highway systems, there were abandoned military vehicles that were spotted as well as field bases to provide a semblance of order to the many refugees that were flooding out of nearby towns or small villages. They passed by farms and ranches as well as the tall metal granary silos, it was eerie to see so much of humanity's achievements sitting idle and it felt like a scene from a movie but that movie had become very much real.

They eventually stopped at the city of Summerville realizing that people needed to rest including those that were driving, it had been a while since they had a bed to rest on or a cot to sleep on. Marcus Wayne helped his family get their things into a gated community as members of the group cleared out the dead inside the homes, when they entered the first home which was cleared out. The home was modern and in the kitchen area it had marble countertops as well as a dining room that had a wooden table that was in the shape of the nation of Middle Earth, Marcus's eyebrow went up seeing their book cases that had multiple copies of Lord of the Rings as well as other things. His wife and son went upstairs as he expanded the home, whomever the homeowner was he clearly loved his favorite movies and had some areas of the room designed to look as if he or she were leaving in Middle Earth. After he walked around the kitchen area as well as the dining area and into the living room did, he climbs the stairs up, from what he was seeing people had lived there before they had arrived. Marcus was a sheriff and had seen signs of a struggle as well as dried blood in the living room, it would be difficult to know what exactly happened or the date or the year when this happened. He stopped before entering the bedroom and saw on a desk in the next room that was to the left of the master bedroom, he stopped and wiped away the dust of the photo to reveal a couple who was young like in their mid to late thirties. The couple according to the photo was a homosexual couple, in the background of the photo it was a ceremony of what he guessed was the adoption of a baby girl. The two men in the photo looked extremely happy and he remembered when his wife as well as himself brought home their son. He smiled before turning his head to the left to see his wife approach him as he was looking at the photo of the gay couple, she joined him and hugged him as she looked at the photo as well seeing how happy they were of welcoming the adoption of their daughter.

"They look so happy together, it reminds me of you and I when we brought Connor into our home. Maybe they managed to leave with their daughter and find a place where they could live." Said Maggie Wayne and saw her husband nod his head before placing the photo back down. He walked into the master bedroom and found his son was fast asleep, the two parents slipped into bed with their son. It was better to sleep in a new environment together and for it to be safety in numbers, the rest of the group settled in the same home as Marcus and his family.

14

CHAPTER 12

It was four days later after the snowstorm had officially passed when Marcus's survivors hit the road on their long journey to Saint Louis Missouri which was hopefully to be the promised land for the group. They had been driving for five hours and had put Summerville behind, they had passed by the other towns before heading to the border of Tennessee. Marcus Wayne had plans that had grown root and stem into his mind, in his mind Saint Louis Missouri was the promise land and they could rebuild what they had lost. Once they arrived, they would scour the landscape for a suitable location for their group as well as an area for future expansion as the population would grow. In his mind he had further plans of the future, once he established the borders of the community and had built outposts to watch the roads or bridges leading to his territory. His mind as he was driving was creating more thoughts for the future once he got his people to Missouri, it was winter and once they got to a place, they would wait out the winter and continue their journey in the spring. The plans remained the same as far keeping his group and his family safe, but the future it was both easy and hard to look forward but the future was expanding as his mind continued his thoughts. In his mind's eye he foresaw his community prospering and there was safety as well as security, his plans included creating a military for his community as a police force and establishing laws. The weather was slowly clearing up but the clouds were not as dark as they were the night before, the sun was trying to break through the winter clouds as if light was battling the darkness of the world. The drive was peaceful except for the occasional repair of the RVs or stopping so people could relieve themselves and the unblocking of roads from some car wrecks, they stopped for fuel as well as scavenge much needed supplies. They passed through small towns that had no name or small farming villages that had no name or history, Marcus's group had seen damaged buildings within these small towns as well as these small farming villages where there were blast craters. He looked in the rearview mirror to see his beautiful wife and his handsome devil of a son sleeping in the back passenger seat, she saw him and smiled at her husband as he returned a wink towards her. He continued driving as he grabbed the radio that was sitting inside the cup holder and turned it on before speaking into the handheld radio.

"Marcus to Carter, How's the weather out there?"

"It's fucking cold out here man, it's like we are in Russia or something. I can't wait until the spring comes, so what's the plan man?"

"We continue pushing until we find a place to stop and we can stay somewhere until the spring before continuing further, I can already see people are getting tired and I would rather people were alert than they weren't alert."

"Yeah alright, we are approaching the border of Tennessee and we should find a place to stay that is close to the city of Nashville." Said Carter as the winter breeze swirled around himself as well as his sister driving the motorcycle next to him, they were like the angels of death on their motorcycle and each had their weapon slung over their shoulder. The convoy of survivors ploughed through the roads like there was no time, the landscape had changed abruptly with the winter weather and it was even more creepy that there were no Christmas decorations.

They continued their drive and passed into Tennessee; however, they drove through Knoxville and it was a hard route to get through. They continued and stopped at Sparta as well as making their campsite at Sparta Hills of Tennessee, the survivors found a nice beautiful house and moved a few supplies into the home where they would be sleeping all together. They had survived Atlanta, the bombing of King James County, the travel to Savannah, the herd that had almost blocked them in Savannah, the battles against the raiders and they were going to survive whatever would be thrown at them or there would be no way out. They were the ones who lived and they were going to be the ones who would rebuild the world better than it was before, it was better to survive together rather than pulling away from each other. Marcus sat in the upstairs office and kept his chair away from the window off to the side, as he remained watchful of the new environment, they were in. He kept the door behind him in his peripheral vision and his primary vision focused on the snow-covered grounds as well as the sniper rifle resting against the wall near the window, he was an excellent marksman and had a perfect eye that aided in his aim as well as seeing threats. He knew his wife was putting their son to bed as well as getting ready for bed herself, they had just eaten and darkness was beginning to cover the sky. In the room opposite his was Randall Welsch in the other room that was once a tv room, downstairs Carter and his siblings were in the living room keeping their eyes as well as ears ready for any threats. Frederick and Rose had set up their quarters in the guest bedroom on the ground floor, the downstairs basement was where they had stored some of the supplies only food, water and medicine as well as fuel for the generators that were located inside the basement. Marcus Wayne was beginning to slowly trust the two new survivors, the rest of those that were recruited in Savannah and had died were buried on the grounds of a church. Marcus's group was getting fewer and fewer, they once had twenty to thirty people but were now down to eleven or twelve survivors. He had seen a lot of death and a lot of destruction in his days as a soldier and an officer, he wanted one day or maybe two or three years when he the experience of true peace. The home that housed the remaining survivors was quiet like a church, the only thing that continued was the howling winds of winter. Marcus felt bad for the children who had survived so much that they only had their moms or their fathers but were afraid of the world around them that they might lose someone else.

Carter Dixon got up from the couch and looked outside to see the snow-covered ground as well as the backyard which at the end had a white fence. He had his crossbow slung over his shoulder and was in a neutral stance, as he used his eyes to scan the area in front of him for threats.

"Hey Carter, do you remember when all this wasn't a thing and we were hanging out that one night? It was your favorite bar in Atlanta and we encountered that homeless man who was preaching about the end of days were upon us, I wonder what ever happened to that crazy fucker and it turns out he was right except the part of Jesus Christ coming back."

"I bet he died preaching to the rotters as they tore him apart and probably using his bible to kill them." Said Atticus Dixon who was laughing as he drank the alcohol inside the home, Martha and Carter were suppressing their laughter knowing that the people who had died by the dead never deserved that fate. Atticus continued to drink the beer bottle in his hands that wasn't cold and was becoming drunk with each passing hour. Carter Dixon walked over to open the front door and saw a rotter approach him, in which he fired his crossbow bolt that penetrated the rotter's skull killing him once again. He walked over to the corpse that was laying in the front yard, he placed his boot against the rotter's skull as he bent down to pull out the crossbow bolt. He heard in the howling wind another rotter that must have smelled a living person to eat, he turned around and dropped his crossbow as he unsheathed his knife in which he brought the blade to the side killing the second rotter. He wondered if there was damage within the community's fenced perimeter or the brick wall, however there were already two dead rotters that were put down. He walked through the snow and kept his eyes focused on the environment around him, his eyes scanned the surrounding environment, he was doing his job as a protector and Marcus's lieutenant. He stopped and saw the brick wall as well as the fence had sustained damage from some sort of weapon, he held onto his knives and froze as he listened carefully to hear the dead that were continuing their snarling as well as moaning. He turned his head to the right to see a house that the windows were boarded up in which the dead were inside, he walked over and investigated the window to see their must have been twenty to maybe thirty rotters inside the house.

"Oh my God." Said Carter as he walked away and headed to the front door to see that it was still intact except for the boards that ran parallel to each other, in Carter's mind it was the early survivors that had herded the dead into this house or the houses that were in the neighborhood. He walked over to the house next door to see that the other house was boarded up and he was able to investigate the windows to see there were rotters inside. It seemed troubling and it seemed that whomever resided here before, had for the safety of the community was to box the dead into two homes, it was smart and it would explain the dead trying to bang on the windows as well as the door to try to escape. He walked back to the house where his group were as well as the vehicles that formed a protective wall of sorts around the house they were staying, the two RVs were parked to the side as well as the motorcycles and the cars. He returned to safety of the home and despite being cold as well as snow on his boots, he walked upstairs to speak to Marcus in private.

Marcus Wayne turned his head and saw that Carter had been out-side probably killing some of the rotters before they got close enough to the house, he turned to the right to the opening of the office and saw Carter enter the office.

"I went outside to kill some rotters that I saw, I decided to do a check of the perimeter and I saw the northern facing brick wall had been damaged at some point as well as the fence. The two houses on this block, whoever lived here before us had placed the dead inside those two homes and had boarded the windows as well as the door. I feel like I may suggest that we find one of the vehicles here that was left behind and maybe drive that vehicle to block the hole in the wall. It should prevent the dead from wandering into that hole, the other thing I noticed while on the road with the group is that the further, we got away from Georgia, the more I noticed we have the common rotters and walkers as well as roamers who move slow not the variants we encountered before."

"Yeah, it's odd, I would assume that these variants would be every-where but the more we leave from the roots of this group. The more that it isn't the case and we run into the same old-fashioned rotter who is slow moving. "said Marcus and took a moment to look outside before switching with Carter to get some sleep. Carter took Marcus's post and the rifle as he opened the window a bit so he could hear better than from the glass in front of him. It was a threat that could wait and the dead were contained inside those homes but the threat that couldn't wait was the brick wall that was damaged and had a hole.

15

CHAPTER 13

It was the next day and the sun had breached through the clouds but it was still cold. Marcus Wayne had woken up early and had found a truck that was parked in the garage of the house they were staying in. Carter Dixon and Randall Welsch lifted the garage door as Marcus Wayne went into reverse down the hill of the house, once he went into reverse and he turned the wheel to the left as he drove around the island and headed to the brick wall in which he drove the vehicle into the hole. He exited the driver side and had blocked the hole, he climbed onto the hood of the car and onto the roof before hopping down to the flatbed before climbing onto solid ground. He smiled as he walked over to the house to see the kids and his son playing with each other as they had a snowball fight. It was nice because in his heart he was feeling for a moment of peace. He walked closer to the house as the snow crunched under the foot of his cowboy boots and the cold wind whipped against his uncovered face. He saw Carter Dixon and Randall Welsch pulled down the garage door together. He walked over and stopped as he crouched and brought his bare hand onto the white snow. It felt so cold and so soft as he made the snow into a little ball in which he threw it at his son who stopped before turning his gaze to his father. Marcus smiled at his son who smiled back before throwing a snowball at his father and the kids joined the fight that was breaking out, it was nothing but laughter and joy as father and son had fun with one another.

Maggie Wayne smiled as she walked on the carpet of their bedroom and saw her husband as well as her son having a snowball fight. It made her smile and it made her feel a small sense of peace knowing that the world is in chaos. She remembered how far she had gotten and how far she had survived. She hoped that would survive till the end when things would go back to a new normal. However, in her personal thoughts she had a deep feeling that she would not survive till the end, she had strength but nowhere in strength of her husband or her son. She felt her stomach churn as if she was about to vomit and ran to the master bedroom's bathroom and began to throw up in the toilet. Once she was finished and cleaned herself up, she went downstairs to speak to Martha who jumped up from her seat and walked over to her.

"Martha, could you do me a favor? I want this between us and nobody else needs to know about this or what I am going to ask of you."

"Yeah sure, what is it Maggie?"

"Could you go to this town's Walgreens or pharmacy and get a pregnancy test for me?

"Yeah, shouldn't Marcus know about you if you feel that you are pregnant."

"No, I don't want to tell him, just please do this for me and I'll be grateful as well as keeping it to yourself." Said Maggie Wayne and saw that Martha had hesitated first in nodding her head, she quickly went to work and got onto her motorcycle outside before driving into town.

While everyone was outside, Randall Welsch walked upstairs and went to Marcus's bedroom where Maggie was dressed in her long sleeved shirt as well as pants. He walked in there and wanted to express that he had hidden feelings for her as well as try to save her from a death that would be directed towards Marcus. He feared that Marcus was leading the group into nothing short but a quick death and he wanted to save them from a foolish death, he walked up to the door that was closed and he knocked the door to be polite. Maggie Wayne answered the door to see Randall was standing in front of her, a little surprised to be sure but not an unwelcome one.

"Hey Randall, do you want something?"

"Yeah, can we talk in private Maggie?"

"Sure, come on in." said Maggie as she opened the door to allow Randall inside who was back to wearing in the warmth of the home his gray t-shirt that clearly defined his muscular form. He walked into the master bedroom and noticed the king size bed as well as a desk where a map was laid out on the surface. The door behind him closed and he looked at Maggie Wayne with nothing but lust in his eyes. Randall Welsch allowed a side of him to come forward and grabbed Maggie Wayne with strength as he threw her to the bed, she struggled to get up and Randall was on top of her removing her clothes forcefully, she tried to scream but her face was pressed into the blankets as Randall forced himself into her. He continued to assault her and rape her until she was in tears begging for him to stop, she used her nails and scratched into his face deeply causing Randall to bleed. In one fluid motion Maggie Wayne kneed Randall in the groin and watched as he stumbled backwards before unholstering her revolver to shoot him. She was in tears and she was hurt both mentally as well as physically after she was raped by a man whom she trusted. Randall backed away from the gun but placed his left hand onto his right cheek where he felt blood running down from the scratch, pain erupted through his cheek as his brain registered the wound that he had sustained. He exited the bedroom and went to his room where he got his coat, before he drove away in his truck to relieve some stress by killing the dead. Once Randall had left, Maggie Wayne cried as she held a pillow so no one could hear her pain.

Randall Wayne drove away from the community and headed further into town where he stopped the car, he grabbed his shotgun that was in the passenger seat next to him from the driver side. He walked away from the truck and cocked the shotgun as he heard the dead banging against the door of a nearby hardware store, his boots crunched on the snow as he approached the door. He opened the door and swung the butt of his shotgun against the head of the rotter that sprung from the door towards him, the sound was loud as the rotter's skull cracked from being hit hard. He stepped over the corpse and fired his shotgun at another rotter who was once a teenager, the body fell with half its skull missing and a massive hole blown away to reveal a portion of his brain. He continued going through the hardware store killing the dead as well as releasing his rage that was growing with every second, once he was finished with the hardware store and there was nothing left but bodies did, he move to the next store as he repeated his wave of carnage. He continued his rampage and was leaving behind corpses as well as a trail of blood that was flowing like a river from the corpses. He knew that some of the survivors within the group had different names for the dead, some of the survivors called the dead rotters, walkers, bloaters, sleepers, climbers, runners, screamers and many other names.

Marcus Wayne headed upstairs and opened the door to the master bedroom to see his wife was in complete disarray, she appeared to be crying and was in distress from something that either happened or was happening.

"Baby, what's wrong? Are you okay?"asked Marcus as he walked slowly towards his wife as she cried, she quickly began to inch away from him not because she was afraid of him but was frightened of what had happened. Marcus asked if Maggie Wayne was okay and realized that her wife was frightened as well as terrified from something that had happened recently. He walked away from the master bedroom because his wife was too upset and didn't want to talk.

CHAPTER 14

Marcus Wayne got up from sleeping on the cot in the office, Randall had returned later the other day in the evening with blood from the dead covering his coat as well as his body. The survivors wondered where he had been all that time and he gave an emotionless reply that he was out hunting the dead, Marcus had been worried as well seeing that his friend or whatever he was now had been killing the dead as if he was serial killer thirsting for the hunt. It was morning and Marcus did his usual routine as he got dressed as he was going to expect the threat that was waiting to come free from the two homes. He went to the dresser and grabbed his belt where his holstered weapon was located, he placed the belt around his waist and rolled his shoulders after sleeping rough on the cot. He then placed his cowboy boots on and fixed his pant legs over his cowboy boots, he knew it was time as he looked on the chair, his sheriff hat as well as the badge that would be given to his son. He gathered the items and walked out of the door to give what belonged to him to his son as a way of passing the torch. He opened the master bedroom to see that his wife was somewhere else in the home and his son was sitting there looking at his booklet from the school.

"Morning Kiddo." Said Marcus as he saw his son beam with happiness and ran over to his father who gave him a big hug. Once they were done hugging each other did Marcus place his sheriff hat on the head of his son as well as place the badge on his son's shirt. His son Connor beamed with happiness as he looked up to see his father's hat on his head as well as his father's badge.

"How's school going kiddo?"

"It's going great daddy; I am learning a lot and one day I am going to run the community like you do daddy." Said Connor as his father was kneeling so he could speak to his son who was nine years old now after his birthday was celebrated in Savannah. Once they were finished talking, Marcus allowed his son to continue working on his homework and to continue his learning to fight the world that was changing around them. He wanted his son to take control of the group if something had happened to him, he knew that he had a role to play as being a leader to his people and surviving till the very end. The adult members of the group agreed that school was always a fundamental part in which children would be formed into the adults that were required in the world tomorrow, except now the children would soon be taught how to use a weapon like knives as well as guns and it was frowned upon but it didn't matter it was quickly overruled. Connor and his friends had brought back the calendar system as well as learning the general stuff from school, Marcus was pleased to see that his son was making friends as well as learning and giving things to the group such as a calendar. He walked out of the house with Carter Dixon, Martha Dixon, Atticus Dixon and Randall Welsch who walked over to the homes that the dead were barricaded inside, the sounds of the dead could be heard some of the way outside. It had stopped snowing but the temperature remained cold, however the sun was breaking through the clouds, soon it would be warm and spring would come through heaven as if God himself was spreading his mercy upon his people. Marcus Wayne didn't believe in God and Jesus Christ; he didn't believe in an afterlife because once somebody died that life is over. He was open minded about the whole religious thing but he doubted a lot of what was spoken about and he believed in the human will to succeed. They arrived at the first home and began to work on clearing them out seeing that Frederick and his wife Rose coming along with a few other adults trained in guns to begin to purge the home of the dead, the plan was to break the wooden boards on the door and open the door to eliminate the threats all together. Marcus Wayne and Carter Dixon used some crowbars that he found inside the shed in the backyard as they ripped the wooden boards off. The rotters inside the home heard the wooden boards being ripped off as they snarled and moaned as their eternal hunger was about to give them a full stomach, once the boards were off, did they slowly open the door. The rotters moved slowly as they exited the home and were being torn apart by Marcus's firing squad, the bullets tore through the dead like it was paper and bodies dropped like stones. The sounds of gunfire crackled around them as the dead were being eliminated, the rotters that were put down fell into the snow as their bodily fluids leaked from the fresh wounds they sustained. Marcus Wayne was hesitating as he saw a child who was four- or five-years old stumble out of the house with a bite mark on her shoulder that was revealed with her torn shirt, he unholstered his Colt Python and walked over to the little girl as he cocked the weapon as he aimed it before firing the killshot between the girl's eyes. He took a moment to process what he had before with shaking hands as he holstered his weapon, he took another moment to calm himself and was sad with how that little girl died and didn't deserve the death.

The corpses of the rotters were double tapped with blades to the head to make sure they were in fact dead and were taken to the home where they were trapped in, the home would serve as their funeral pyre to be burned. Carter and Marcus used some propane tanks that they found as well as an empty gas can that was spreading throughout the home after they poured the liquid throughout the home, then once they were cleared did, they light a match from the second floor and as it spread through the home like wildfire did Frederick and Rose whisper to themselves but loud enough to be heard a prayer for the souls still trapped in the rotters. The first home was successfully cleared of the rotters and slowly the flames began to engulf the home as thick black smoke began to spill outwards. They had the other home to deal with and the dead would be put to rest like the others that have come in the path of the group, near the other home the blood had erased the pure white snow as the blood mixed with the snow as the flames danced in the first home. The process continued until the second home was cleared and the bodies were collected to be burned, Randall and Atticus both as well as Frederick poured gas in its liquid form throughout the home to burn the corpses inside. Once the threat was removed and the two homes that were burned had fallen into ruin as if it was a battlefield in the history textbooks. The entire country looked to be a warzone and a battlefield as Marcus's group trailblazer from where they started in Atlanta to Savannah, to Charleston South Carolina as well as North Charleston before driving through Summersville and eventually reaching where they were now in Sparta Hills Kentucky. The world belonged to the dead and it was up to a small group of survivors to try to change everything and to try to bring the world back to the living. They hoped that in the future that was to come that it was humanity who had reclaimed their world as they would try to rebuild everything. Marcus Wayne wondered what had happened to his wife, he hoped he hadn't done anything to her or neglected her in any way. He knew his wife would speak to him when she was ready to speak, however as a former officer of the law and having a deep knowledge of how to read people. It troubled him and knew not to push questions when they weren't feeling up to speaking and he was worried for her. He walked around a bit and then decided to head back inside as the others were heading back inside to get warm while the Dixon siblings were grabbing some firewood to get another fire going inside the home. Once the evening rolled around and the firewood was gathered that was then placed into the fireplace to be burned to provide heat. Marcus Wayne sat next to his nine-year-old son with whom he was well pleased, he was becoming intelligent and slowly with the teachings from Carter and Martha Dixon on how to hunt as well as the lessons of self defense from his father he was becoming stronger every day. They were sitting amongst the fireplace getting warm as they were eating some canned food as well as drinking water from bottles, Marcus looked to the right to see that his wife was sitting away from everyone else and only sat next to her husband to get warm. Once they finished eating the food and drinking some water as well as getting warm from sitting by the fireplace did, they all fell asleep.

17

—·—

CHAPTER 15

It had been a year since they had survived the trails of Atlanta and the raiders in the farm near Savannah as well as the snowstorm, they were gathering their stuff to leave Sparta Hills Kentucky in preparation for spring but something still wreaked havoc within Marcus's mind of the silence of his wife and the deep scratch marks on Randall's right cheek. He and Randall decided to go for a drive as they would be going 18 miles out to see the route that they would be heading to Saint Louis. Marcus Wayne and Randall Welsch drove a ford edge vehicle as Marcus sat on the driver side as Randall's seat was the passenger seat. The car's radio was playing some country music and something was telling Marcus that something had happened between his wife and Randall. As they drove Marcus pulled over to the side of the road and put the vehicle in park as he let the engine run. "Now is your chance Randall to be honest to me, I saw my wife and she looked like she was violently assaulted by someone. She doesn't talk to me and doesn't want to be near me, so I want the truth that something happened that I need to know about and if you're honest with me then I may forgive you depending on the severity but if it is severe then I will throw you out of this group." "Nothing happened man, she must have had a mental breakdown and started breaking stuff. I came there to help her calm down and she scratched me so I put her in handcuffs until she calmed down. After I left, I don't know what occurred next." Said Randall as he lied to his friend's face that it was himself who raped his friend's wife and violently attacked her, Marcus nodded his head as what he was told rolled in his head but his story wasn't adding up that Randall handcuffed her and their marks from handcuffs on her arms. "Except there is one problem with your story, there weren't marks from handcuffs on her wrists on both arms. The area around the back of her neck was red as if someone held her down in the bedroom, her face was still somewhat red. It told me things even without her speaking it and I had a feeling that she was raped as well as sexually assaulted. "said Marcus as he looked at Randall with eyes that a hawk would look at too its prey before killing it, after a while of looking at his friend who remained calm drove the car off the side of the road. In the mind of Marcus, he knew that Randall was lying to him and it was a matter of time when his wife would speak to him. He continued to drive as he approached a small town that was a farming community and parked the car near the local elementary school. The two of them exited the car as Marcus turned the car off as well as taking the keys which he placed into his pants pocket, the two of them walked over to the fence of the Elementary school which was once a national guard field hospital. They saw that behind the fence and on the school property, there were empty military structures such as vehicle repair workshops and some barracks as well as some clinics. They saw rows of parked helicopters and vehicles that sat motionless, there were clear signs that this also served the purpose of the military as an outpost.

"We don't know how many of the dead are inside or if there are any survivors inside, I think we should do this quiet no guns only knives."

"Alright man, but we have guns and bullets, why can't we use them."

"Because like I told you in Savannah, guns are loud and they attract the dead. If we want to move quietly and with speed it means blades, Randall take it from a guy who was in the military and has done a lot of stuff by using knives to eliminate threats. Since you taught me how to kill the dead and how to avoid groups of them, I'll show you how to use stealth and how to move quietly. The thing about stealth is not to be quick, but to slow the thing moving and you take your time as you eliminate threats." Said Marcus went into his left pocket to pull out his switchblade and opened the blade as he cut the palm of his left hand to see blood starting to flow out of the wound, he smeared his blood against the metal fence before shaking it causing the metal to clank. They waited for a few minutes before they heard a rotter approach, probably smelling blood of a fresh kill from his zombie brethren. The rotter was wearing a suit and tie as if he was once a businessman, Marcus used his knife and plunged the blade deep into the skull of the rotter seeing the life leave his corpse. He pulled the blade and saw that Randall had done the same by cutting his palm as he killed a rotter who was dressed in the clothes of a doctor. The two listened for a moment before climbing the fence and entering the grounds, when they got some distance from the bodies of the two dead rotters and saw that the military had completely converted the elementary school into an outpost as well as a medical treatment facility. They found the all too familiar logos of the CDC and United States military, it looked as if the outpost was another battleground by the military against the dead that they were trying to contain. They were there to scout out the road as well as clear out any nearby buildings that contained the dead, they knew that it was a new year and spring was approaching which meant they could continue their journey to Saint Louis.

"Somebody help me!" shouted a man from the distance as both Marcus and Randall looked at each other before sprinting in the direction of a person screaming in fear, the training in both Marcus and Randall of being a sheriff kicked back into high gear as they heard that someone needed assistance. Marcus and Randall both not caring about using stealth but to save someone fired their guns as they watched the dead fall with bullet holes in their heads as they saw a man who was wearing a coat on top of a trash dumpster. They pulled the man who was wearing a coat and they saw that his pants resemble those of what a prisoner would wear, Marcus went for his back pouch as he placed his handcuffs on the man for his own safety. Randall pointed his pistol at the man who was terrified to see a weapon pointing at him and was even more afraid of the hell that he was in before. Marcus searched the man and placed the knife he found on the snowy ground as well as a key to a car onto the ground. He was curious about where this person was located before coming here.

"Who are you?"

"I....my...name....is...Lucas...sir."

"Okay so Lucas, where did you come from?"

"Could.... you.... lower...that...weapon?" asked Lucas he saw Randall was pointing his pistol and lowered the weapon when Marcus placed a calm hand on the weapon to lower it. He could tell that the man was terrified and was a young man in his late twenties. He waited for Lucas to collect himself before waiting for him to answer the question, Randall kept his eyes moving as he searched the surroundings for any sign of the dead coming. "I'm from Saint Louis sir, well not originally, I lived in Kansas City and I ran into this group that took me in. Everything was fine and then the leader of the group changed as they became more ruthless. I spoke out against the group and I was sent to the Saint Louis Prison where we did hard labor as well as getting beaten by the guards. The man in charge of the Saint Louis Prison calls himself the Warden and he calls himself the mayor within the community. The group within the community is around 660 people and there are around forty-five people who are in that prison, the leader is fucking crazy man. I escaped from that prison by knocking out one of the guards, then I got to the fence and sprinted until I was a good distance away before finding a car where I drove to Kentucky but ran out of gas. The leader he killed my parents by hanging them in front of the citizens of the town he has walled off, he raped my two sisters as he made me watch and then he made me watch as he strangled my sisters to death. He hung their lifeless bodies like they were Jesus Christ and he then arrested me for being a traitor. I want to free those people and I was once a good scout as well as a supply runner." Said Lucas as desperation crept into his voice to be able to survive with a group was a blessing rather than being alone. "I understand Lucas, you can have a place with us but you need to prove yourself and you must earn my trust. We were heading to Missouri once spring arrived and since you know the layout, we could find a place where we could build our base of operations." "Of course." Said Lucas as he saw that Randall was giving a snort of derision not too pleased of Marcus opening the gates, Lucas voluntarily had the blindfold wrapped around his eyes as they left heading back to the cars hearing that the dead inside the school were banging the doors trying to get out.

18

CHAPTER 16

M arcus honked his horn outside of the gated community with the blindfolded Lucas sitting in the back passenger seat with his hands bound in front of him, he felt bad for him that he watched his family to be killed in front of him as well as his sisters being raped in front of him before watching them die. He knew from that his friendship was on the rocks with Randall because of him taking leadership over the group as well as working side by side with his people, the gate opened and he drove through seeing that the two homes were burned down and were nothing but black as space itself. Marcus exited the driver car as he opened the back passenger door and grabbed Lucas who followed his every instruction when instructed, he heard Randall follow behind him into the home where Lucas was brought down to the basement. Marcus knelt and handed the items that he searched from Lucas to Randall who walked away, he removed the blindfold and smiled at him.

"You're going to save with us, we do this because we have children in our group and we are just being careful."

"I understand sir, thank you." Said Lucas as he saw Marcus walk upstairs from the basement into the first floor. Lucas for the first time was beginning to feel safe and his feelings led him to the conclusion that Randall had a darkness inside him that was growing stronger. Lucas's mother told him that everyone has energy that people could read and determine if that person was a man or a woman of light or darkness, his mother was once a psychic and was a very religious person. Marcus walked over to the garage to see that Atticus was working on adjusting his motorcycle, it was time for something that was bothering him to be brought into the light. He closed the garage door that led into the home and saw that Atticus was aware of somebody being in the room with him, he walked over and stood over Atticus like a dark shadow.

"I want you to answer truthfully about what happened to those raiders when I let them go, your brother and your sister as well as those that I brought with me saw the accident that had occurred. The blood and the oil mixing together as well as clear signs of a struggle, I want to know the truth where you and Randall as well as those that followed you went after you departed. I think you know something and that you fear Randall because you were with him when the raiders were very much alive. "

"Okay, I'll tell you because I am frightened and I have done a lot of bad things in my life. I killed people, I was in gangs and I was a drug dealer. I want to become a better person and I want to make amends with my siblings because I made their jobs harder by having a little brother who was a criminal." "I understand Atticus, tell me what happened that day after leaving the farm before I did."

"Randall, myself and the others that were with us drove away. We followed the raiders off road and knew the route they were using, we set up a trap and we waited. We used some spikes and the cars drove over them causing a wreck to occur. Then we went into there and it was a slaughter, I saw Randall and he was enjoying it. He is becoming pure evil and he's told me in private that he wants to become the leader as well as take your family away from you. He hasn't told if he wants to kill you or anyone else, but I don't know but I think he is becoming a psychopath in the making and I never saw a man who was enjoying killing someone. He strangled that leader and allowed a rotter to bite into that man's face. I'm sorry Marcus, I just can't be hanging around him anymore and I feel like you are the better leader than he was because we wouldn't be around."

"It's okay Atticus, the truth can set you free and I've been seeing things that you have seen but have kept hidden. We have a chance now to correct things in our lives that we felt were horrible things, I think you know that the former you, the criminal, must die now so that the new person could rise from the ashes."

"I understand Marcus, thank you. I wish I knew you when I was younger because you could have changed things from turning out how they did. But I know that you speak true because it feels like a weight was lifted off my chest." Said Atticus who wiped away the tears knowing that his old ways were going must die for himself to become a better person. Marcus walked away and back into the home; he was armed with the truth that Randall was hiding from him. Marcus was concerned that their friendship was over with Randall, but he would wait to ask his wife what had occurred because something told him that Randall was also behind it. He went back into the home and closed the door behind him to leave Atticus in peace, He went to a closet where the former homeowners had stored extra pillows and blankets as he grabbed them before heading down to the basement where Lucas would be sleeping. Once getting the items, he walked over and opened the basement door as he walked the stairs to the basement which was a finished construction that also included its own bedroom as well as bathroom. He went over to Lucas who was glad to see Marcus and freed him from the handcuffs before walking with him to the basement guest bedroom. "

Come on Lucas, I'll give you a room and tomorrow we will be getting ready to leave for Saint Louis. I would like to speak to you later tonight by looking at the map and if you could mark out the territory of this Warden, what is his real name Lucas?" "

His name is Philip Scott; he was the former mayor of Saint Louis and has a history as being a well-respected warden. I remember that his wife and son had died in a car crash or they were murdered, the details of that were a little fuzzy but I remember something happened with them. Thank you for not killing me or hurting me sir, I am happy that you are going to give me a chance to join your group of survivors."

"Your welcome Lucas, what happened to your family and what you saw was an act of pure evil. This man Philip Scott I don't want to go into a war if I'm not provoked first or attacked first, violence is a means to an end when all other options have been worn out. I have been in war and I was a sheriff before all this, I was shot on duty in 2008 when responding to a bank robbery. We lost a lot of officers that day and I was close to death, but I survived, because we are the ones who live. Your family will never truly be gone because their memories are in your heart and you still have the lessons of your father. Come on, I have the map in my back pocket so let's mark the territory of that guy before you forget as well as his outposts if he has any."

"Okay sir." Said Lucas as he followed Marcus into the spare bedroom and helped him set up his room before laying out the map on a desk as well as giving a pen to Lucas so he could mark out the landscape. Marcus watched as Lucas marked out the map and clearly marked the area that the warden had control of was in control of Saint Charles Corrections as well as the town he controlled was Wentzville. The map also had marked areas that were outposts for Philip Scott's group, Lucas informed Marcus that Saint Louis was a warzone by the national guard and the dead that it was a bloodbath. Lucas knew plenty of information of how the local criminals fought alongside the police as well as the military in order to keep the overwhelming hordes of the dead from getting further into the city, however the military pulled out and blew up two bridges but the third bridge was damaged and never destroyed. Marcus knew that the military had done something horrible by leaving those people to die, they had orders and swore an oath of allegiance to protect the nation as well as its people from its enemies.

"Thank you, Lucas, now get some rest and you are safe now. You have nothing left to fear anymore." Said Marcus as he placed a fatherly hand onto the young man's shoulder who smiled knowing that he was safe from the evils of a man who brutalized him. Marcus departed after seeing Martha Dixon bring Lucas a meal as well as a water bottle, the evening went smooth and soon it was light's out for everyone while some survivors worked in shifts to start the loading process of the supplies for their journey. However, Marcus slept with his wife who was clearly fragile after something was done to her, their son Connor slept on the floor with his father's hat next to him as well as his father's sheriff badge.

19

CHAPTER 17

Three months, two weeks, seven days had passed since staying within the confines of Sparta Kentucky. The survivors once the snow and ice had melted began to slowly drive out of the gated community, they were now up to twenty-three survivors but many of those that were with them had died in the camping site near Atlanta as well as the city of Savannah. Those numbers were now substantially less where they were thirty-nine to maybe forty strong but were now reduced to a shadow of that force, those parents had left behind their sons as well as daughters in the care of people who would be complete strangers in years prior but had become family. Marcus's power base had grown to now include Atticus Dixon who had admitted his faults in the massacre of the raiders who were defeated but were killed because Randall believed his former best friend was weak. Marcus had gathered Carter Dixon, Martha Dixon and Atticus who he worked to repair a family that was fractured from the past that needed to be burned for a healthy bond to form. Marcus Wayne, Carter Dixon, Martha Dixon, Lucas and Atticus Dixon before leaving went back to the elementary school to clear out the buildings which they were horrified to see the bloodbath that occurred years prior in the chaos of the collapse. Marcus and his family left behind the vehicle they had used since Atlanta that wouldn't run anymore, where they boarded the RV where Frederick and his wife Rose were there as well as Lucas. The driver he never really met but had survived in Atlanta was in the front seat, he was very quiet and didn't really speak a lot.

The convoy of the survivors began to roll out of a place they called home for the last part of the winter season but were looking ahead to the road of Saint Louis where Marcus being the leader had told his people of a dangerous group that was in the place they were heading, but he promised them that he would only defend his people if they were attack and they would be looking for a place to live. The survivors for the first time in what felt like centuries had seen the sun shining in the sky as well as nature beginning to come back to life, it was the last time that they would be seeing the valleys and hills of Kentucky and recorded in the memory of their minds to block out everything they had survived. Marcus sat on a booth as he was cleaning his gun and as well as conducting his many rituals he did within the military; he checked and rechecked his equipment as well as marked off the map whenever they had passed. His son was amazed as his father conducted the many rituals that soldiers would do before going off into battle. "Hey dad, where did you learn how to do so many things at the same time?"

"Well, it's something that I will teach you one day, you remember when I told you that daddy was in the military and they taught him a lot of skills to prepare him when the time came." "Yeah, I do, is that where you learned how to do those things?"

"Yeah, I did, when you get older, I will teach you because one day you will become the leader of these people so you would need to know how to handle things at the same time."

"Awesome daddy, but you will always be the leader dad." Said Connor as he smiled at his father who smiled back with nothing but love showing in his eyes. Once he was finished with cleaning his gun, he put it back into his holster as well as using his radio to monitor the chatter as the Dixons were the vanguard as well as running point for the convoy. He was happy to bring about a peace agreement between that family and they had forgiven Atticus for his wrong doings as well as his faults in the past knowing that it stemmed from the lack of love their family gave them. Marcus looked out the window to see abandoned farms where farmers would be planting the first seeds for the next corps to be grown, but it was silent and the only thing that he could see walking around the farm was the rotters who were joining in a feeding frenzy of an animal they had killed. It was nature taking its course but there was nothing natural about the dead coming back to life to feed on the living, it felt as if it was a horror movie that had become something real or as if the reality, they once lived wasn't an actual reality like it was a dream but they all knew that it wasn't a dream because that was wishful thinking. The survivors traveled on Sparta Pike and then took the ramp on the left as they drove on I-71 south towards Louisville, a couple of hours passed and drove past Louisville before making a right on the ramp on I-64 west toward Saint louis as they moved slowly to avoid the vehicles that were piled up heading in the direction of Louisville which was once another safe zone before it feel like all the rest. They then exited route 64 on the 96 before heading left on I-64 where they continued before towards Saint Louis but stopped as they made it over to a gas station to refuel, as well as for the survivors to relieve themselves before continuing their journey using the backroads to avoid the dead.

They stopped when the RV that contained Marcus and his family as well as Frederick, Rose and the orphaned children due to the age of the RV was bound to continue to break down. The driver and Atticus Dixon worked on the RV to find that the engine had overheated and it needed water to cool the engine, Marcus and the other survivors stopped driving as they parked their vehicles next to those that were abandoned. The sun was clearly shining and it was getting hot, however that didn't eliminate the risks of being out in the open for too long. Marcus got up on the roof of the RV that was being repaired, which was the nickname of RV one, he had in his hands a semi-automatic sniper rifle that had a suppressor attached to the barrel. He slung the sniper rifle over his shoulder and looked at the binoculars to see his people were going into the abandoned cars to gather supplies such as some canned goods as well as medical supplies if they could find them, it appeared from what they were seeing was that the highways were slowly clogging up and there was a panic when they either saw the massive hordes of the dead before causing further panic as well as wrecks to use the backroads. He took a moment to look through the binoculars and saw nothing, however it was moments after he looked again when the RV's engine gave a screeching sound as the water was being poured to cool it. He looked quickly through the binocular's lenses to see a small herd of rotter's number two hundred of the undead were slowly walking towards the sound they heard, they were either close by or they had heard it when they were roaming around.

"Everybody get under cars, remain silent. Carter looked north and spread the word." Said Marcus in a hushed whisper but could be heard as he threw the binoculars in which Carter caught it to see what Marcus had seen, causing him to tell people who didn't hear to get under the cars. The survivors wherever they were and went under the cars that had long been abandoned except for their occupants who had either killed themselves or had turned before being put down by the military or someone else. Marcus had his belly to the rough of the RV as everything had went silent as he took peeks here and there to see another herd had begun to merge with the first herd, he had seen that began walking on the road as if the dead had begun to appear from the woods in the hopes of a feeding frenzy. Randall Welsch and Martha Dixon hid underneath an old State trooper patrol car, its occupant an officer who was still slouched in his driver seat had appeared to have killed himself and the person who was in the back still wearing her cuffs had turned before starving or some other fate. They heard the rotter herd as they shuffled as they walked as well as their constant moans, they snarled and the smell of them was horrible as they got a whiff of what a rotting corpse smell like. They had smelled the dead when they fought them up close and personal, it was a clear smell of a rotting corpse as well as the smell of fecal matter in their pants as they were not in control of their bowels. Martha covered her mouth to prevent herself from gagging and causing a noise as well as Randall who placed his hand over his mouth but realized his shotgun was away from him but still had his holstered Glock.

The rotter herd moved slowly as their feet shuffled on the pavement, their decaying corpses was overpowering of rot as well as the sounds of their snarling or moaning was almost deafening. Marcus from time to time peered over of the roof of the RV and saw the dead moving past the vehicles that were moved or were already away from the roadway, they bumped into the cars which caused for some of the car alarms to go off which caused other rotters from the woods to join the herd as they moved from the survivors who were hidden. The survivors remained motionless while they hid and waited as the herd of the dead moved away as they continued to walk, the rotter's clothes were from various walks of life and there were small males as well as females and children that had died who turned. The survivors waited for a moment once the herd had walked away before getting up and finishing the repairs of the engine of the first RV before continuing their journey, Marcus crouched on the roof of the RV and watched the herd as they walked into the woods heading to a direction where God only knew where they were going. He looked through the scope of the sniper rifle and aimed at a rotter tempted to take the shot but knew they wouldn't hear it due to the suppressor attached to the barrel, he decided on himself that he would take the shot and fired at two rotters who were far away from the herd that were killed with precise headshots. Once the survivors finished the repairs Marcus climbed down from the roof and joined his family who had come out of hiding when he entered the vehicle, and the convoy continued their journey to Saint Louis. Marcus sat down and turned the handheld radio on as he continued listening to the communications of the survivors who were calling out things on the road that could damage the vehicles causing them to go off road for a bit before hopping back on the road.

"Carter, do you think that the dead are migrating or emigrating from other countries that fell during the collapse?" asked Marcus on the radio thinking something that was in mind noticing that there were some of the dead that he killed were from other countries in terms of how they had dressed.

"Yeah, I guess so are they floating from the ocean or crossing the borders. I noticed in that herd that some of the dead had uniforms from the Mexican police as well as the Canadian police, it looks like they merge into herds or hordes that move in a singular fashion but once whatever noise had traveled so far then they split going off in different directions."

"It's interesting and guess they go wherever the soundwaves have attracted their attention as they head in that direction." Said Marcus as he finished another thought that had come into his mind noticing that the dead would cluster into another herd as they walked around until there was a noise which would attract more attention. The road was going to be long but they were heading in the right direction and the survivors knew of the group that Lucas ran away from as a so-called Warden but was a warlord, that they would defend themselves if attacked by them. The survivors stopped to get some rest at Wayne Fitzgerald State Park and cleared out the main office where they would be sleeping for the night. They were so close and they had survived so much that would break people before the journey even began. They had arrived at Illinois and they were so close to their journey coming to an end in Missouri.

20

CHAPTER 18

In the early Morning, preparations continued for them to leave as they packed up the supplies that they used the night before as they were eating canned food. Marcus walked over to a quiet place and crouched down as he saw the water below him on the lake. He took a deep breath as a sense of peace came over him as the world began to change from winter to spring. He heard the water lapping against the rocks as well as hitting the docks where there were rows of boats that would be waiting for their owners for a longtime, he could imagine in the years that passed before the collapse of people coming to this park to enjoy the peace of nature before returning to the chaos of nature. He smiled to himself knowing that he had survived so much and was thankful for his training from the military for giving him the tools that would be needed again as well as the police training he received once going to the academy. He hoped his brother and his sister were okay wherever they were as well as his cousins if they were safe trying to survive this world, he knew that his brother and sister were tough and that they were probably surviving. It was a constant battle wherever they tried to stay they had to leave because threats were beginning to mount either from the weather or the dead, now they had to worry about the living which became apparent with the battle against the raiders away from Savannah and now Marcus knew that war would happen again with the Warden. But when that time came to fight the warden, he would and he needed to bind his strength but be ever watchful. Marcus got up after looking at the lake and walked over to the RV where his family had boarded on it, they still had a good distance before arriving in Saint Louis and it was time to push forwards.

The survivors pulled out of Wayne Fitzgerald Park and began to turn onto the road they had traveled from the night before, the vehicles had their high beam lights on as they drove seeing some of the snow but was melting as the world began to awake after winter came. They drove on State Highway 154 until they reached the town of Sesser before continuing onwards, the town had shared the same fates as the others they had seen from Georgia, to South Carolina as well as Kentucky where they were damaged or war torn. They were on time as Marcus marked off where they had been as he made a record of the travel.

Marcus hoped at this rate that within a couple of hours or by the afternoon, they would arrive at one of the bridges into Saint Louis where Marcus would use his binoculars to see if the route as far as he could see was open. They reached an intersection where they decided to take US highway 51 until they reached State Road 15 where they made a left to continue down the road. They stopped one or two times along the way on State Road 15 where they refueled as they continued through the small city of Washington County IL before continuing through a small-town St. Libory which was in St. Clair County where they eliminated a small group of rotters. They paused for a moment where they relieved themselves as well as eating something from their canned food supplies which was slowly being drained and the supplies of freshwater.

After they had taken their break, they continued and they were slowly getting tired from the constant driving as they felt like they were a defeated army returning. By the early afternoon of what seemed like centuries being on the road reached the very borders of Saint Louis Missouri, the Gateway Arch greeted them but was badly damaged from what appeared to be some sort of crash from a plane that clipped the structure before crashing into the city proper. They exited their vehicles and waited for when Marcus would use his binoculars to locate a route into the city. They were tired but there was a sense of joy at finally reaching their destination.

21

CHAPTER 19

The survivors waited as they watched each other's back and eliminated the rotters that came towards them with blades instead of guns. Marcus cleared out the church by himself with ease, he used his knife with speed as well as purpose delivering quick blows to the head that killed the rotters. He walked over to a doorway as he climbed up the stairwell towards the bell tower, he had his binoculars in his other hand which was a left hand as he used the knife in the right hand. Once he reached the bell tower, he looked through the eye lenses of the binoculars towards the city of Saint Louis and it was war torn like Atlanta was as well as Louisville. He looked down below him to see that his group were killing the dead that came towards them and leaving behind corpses as they slashed and stabbed the rotters, he smiled seeing them work together and effectively as a group. He resumed his focus as he investigated the binoculars to see that Macarthur

Bridge was destroyed from the National Guard, Popular Street Bridge was damaged but was crossable and Martin Luther King Bridge was destroyed, the city appeared to be empty and there were barely any signs of the dead roaming around which told him they either moved on or followed the survivors as they returned away from the city. He stopped before walking down the stairwell as he looked towards the direction of Alton Illinois to see something that resembled a helicopter like the one he saw a longtime ago. He froze as he saw the helicopter stop and hover over the city as if the pilot was staring at Marcus but that was impossible, he watched as the helicopter flew away.

"What the fuck? Is the military still out there?" asked Marcus to himself but shook his head to file what he saw in his mind so people didn't think he was crazy before. He took a moment to collect himself before walking down the marble staircase and exiting the church seeing the corpses of the dead he killed as their blood leaked onto the marble floor, the rotters were a mixed bunch of African Americans, Asian Americans and White Americans who were killed when they looked to God for answers or to stop this from happening. He walked and his cowboy boots echoed along the marble walls as he took a moment to walk over to the altar where he saw the crucifix. He felt like a stranger being in a church, he wasn't religious and didn't believe in God but he wanted to test what those people believed in or if he was even real.

"I don't know if you exist or if you're even real. But I guess you know that your so-called children are struggling to survive in this world where the dead are walking. I respect what you give people a sense of purpose after you die but I don't know if I believe it. If you are real maybe you could give us a sign of, I don't know people not being afraid and that you give us our world back, I've also seen what happens when you use your words to an end for violence. I've killed people before and I put my faith somewhere else instead of a church or a book that was written before this ever happened. If you want to prove your existence to me, then send your angels to cleanse the earth of the dead." Said Marcus to the crucifix where he saw Jesus Christ, he walked away and exited the church knowing where they were headed to get into the city. Before he decided to leave, he gave his group some time to rest and to gather their strength before making their final push before they set up camp where they could wait for whatever they were planning on doing next. Marcus followed his wife as she walked into the church that he was in moments ago, he knew that this was the time to ask her what happened to her a year before during the winter months.

Marcus walked over to his wife Maggie who was kneeling at the altar praying to God for guidance, he thought to himself that at least she had faith and he hoped that helped her.

"Babe, you don't have to say anything but I am worried for you. Did you get hurt or harassed? You aren't yourself and I am worried for you."

"You failed me Marcus, you told me that you fucking protect me and our son but you let the fucking monster into the hen house." Said Maggie as she sprung to her feet and looked at Marcus with tears beginning to fall from her eyes, he saw the fear and the anger in her eyes that wasn't directed towards him but was focused on him.

"What happened? Did someone hurt you?!"

"Randall your friend raped me and sexually assaulted me. He knocked on the door and said he wanted to talk until the next thing I knew I was thrown on the bed with my face being forced down into the pillow as I felt his penis penetrate me. I tried to scream but it was muffled as he forced more head into the pillow and held me there until he was done." Said Maggie Wayne as she began to cry uncontrollably and she allowed her husband to hug her which felt like centuries had gone past when it was only ten minutes where she began to gather herself before speaking to her husband with something he didn't want to do because it was the living against the dead.

"Marcus, Randall is dangerous and it is clear that he wants to take control of the group but I think he wants to take possession of me. That much was clear when he raped me and I don't know if he is jealous of you or us but its clear he wants the leadership. Marcus, Randall at some point needs to die and I am not asking you do that but he hasn't been the same since the collapse." Said Maggie as she kissed her husband on the lips, he kissed back but kept his eyes open while hers were closed with nothing but anger as well as malice in his eyes. The part of him being a soldier and a husband with the promises he told her about protecting her was coming forth from the vows he took to her after they were married to protect her. By the early evening, the survivors decided to stay the night within the National Shrine of our Lady of Snow.

22

EPILOGUE

Staff Sergeant Dunn was promoted to Corporal Dunn, he was former United States Army and he still wore his uniform except for when the flag of his country was altered. The patch with his flag was the United States flag but it completely changed, the stars were removed and the blue spot was a void. The red and white stripes on the flag were no longer showing color but instead in the middle of those stripes was the five circles that were in front of two M4 rifles that were behind the five circles that formed an x. The planned succession state of the United States was formed shortly after the country fell and the dead roamed the earth bringing down the nations of the living, he was in Atlanta when things went south and the shit hit the fan. He had grown a beard and was walking through the mountain base that was in fact an old United States fallout shelter that was used now by the succession state. Dunn walked past twenty to maybe thirty sentries that were standing guard in the various hallways and standing outside metal doors, the new banner hanging from the rock ceiling as well as on the metal scaffolds. The soldiers were wearing their old uniforms but there were slight changes to the uniform, there were portions that were being upgraded with flame resistant as well as zombie bite resistant. The uniforms were being upgraded with a mixture of silk and leather which would give a feeling of it being lighter. The military or what remained of it had gone underground with what remained of the United States Government and the American corporate entities as well as what remained of the scientists plus the medical world. Dunn walked into a room that served as the intelligence and or command center of the Civic Federal Republic Military, he entered the room as the two sentries stepped aside, they were armed with assault rifles and even their guns were being upgraded. Dunn entered the room and saw a table in the middle of the room that served as where the officers as well as commanders would look at the map of the United States as their patrols from the air mapped out the cities that were filled with the dead. Dunn and everyone else reminded what was going on as if the show the Walking Dead was coming to life or had come to life in front of their eyes, Dunn saw that the map had been updated since he was last inside the room, the lights were almost too bright and it felt like Dunn was staring into the sun. He placed his arms against the table as he studied the map and saw markings as well as rough estimations of what was occurring within the cities on the map of the United States. Dunn saw the rough estimations of the dead that were in San Francisco, Seattle, Dallas, San Antonio, Saint Louis and many other cities and towns, the city of Tampa in Florida was reportedly nuked from the United States navy resulting in the deaths of thousands or millions.

"So, you get a look at the map, Corporal Dunn."

"Yeah, I am Luke. I am looking forward to when we will leave this place and go back out there in the fight as well as help people again. The United States failed and this new government will have the strength to defend its people as well as destroy the dead. When everything is finished, we will rebuild this planet in our own image and things will be brought to order. I hear we have a city in mind that should serve us as our capital city and the powerbase of our new government."

"Yeah, I heard the same thing and I found out about the city from Lieutenant Richard Wayne. In the coming months and the coming weeks, we will be leaving a small garrison here and the rest of us will be leaving for Philadelphia. The city fell to the dead; however, the dead left the city as they migrated somewhere else." Said Luke who was a former Central Intelligence Agent, his wife worked at the British embassy as well as a former British Secret service agent. Dunn nodded and turned his head to the right as he looked to see the city of Philadelphia where it was marked on the map with a star showing it was marked to become a capital. It was time for them to hit back, throughout the government fallout bunker which was built into the mountain was a vast complex of tunnels as well as corridors and facilities that were underground. Also, on the map was marked the secondary capital city which was Pittsburg, the plan would be hard and there would be casualties but it was for the greater good. Dunn had received his new assignment four months ago of going near Washington DC where he would blend in with a community.

23

Author's Note

Hi everyone, I just wanted to thank you as well as everyone for reading this book. I hope that you liked this book and enjoy the storytelling as much as I enjoyed writing it. I have some interesting things coming to you with the second book and expand the world of Survive or Die as we take a journey together. I took inspiration from things and I before writing this book used my mind as I cooked new ideas before shaping them on paper, I took a lot of time and a lot of effort to build this into something that I would hope people would enjoy as well as find entertaining. I am looking forward to writing the second book as we explore together a post zombie apocalyptic Saint Louis Missouri, where we will see more zombies and the struggles of leadership in the eyes of Marcus as he tries to keep his moral code in check. I will say that there might be a shocking death or two in the Saint Louis Story arc, because as of finishing this book I am working on both the second and third book as well as story plotting the fourth book. I am planning on some things for the second book, either a time jump like three years or four years. But I just wanted to say thank you and remember we survive or we die. The other thing as well that I wanted to speak on was that Marcus Wayne was born in 1983 of October 10th and within this new year of which being 2012 he is 28,

Connor I meant to change his age from being four or five but be seven or eight but by now he is nine years old. I hope that you look over that because I just realized that and you know sometimes whenever you are writing it's like watching a movie in your head as you type. But anyway, I look forward to the many years of exploring this series and thank you for your comments as well as your thoughts. I welcome criticism because it makes me a better writer.

Thank you to everyone John McGauley